STRIPES

of the **SIDESTEP**

WOLF

SONYA HARTNETT

Copyright © 1999 Sonya Hartnett

First U.S. paperback edition in this format 2019

The Library of Congress has cataloged the hardcover edition as follows:

Hartnett, Sonya.
Stripes of the sidestep wolf / by Sonya Hartnett. —1st U.S. ed.
p.   cm.
Summary: Satchel O'Rye, devoted son of an impoverished couple in a dying rural town, must weigh in balance the life of his most cherished dog and the freedom of a mysterious rare animal.
Children's book council of Australia short-listed book.
ISBN 978-0-7636-2644-0 (hardcover)
[1.Poverty—Fiction. 2. Dogs—Fiction.
3. Family life—Australia—Fiction. 4. Australia—Fiction.
5. Thylacine—Fiction. 6. Rare animals—Fiction.]   I. Title.
PZ7.H267387St 2005 [Fic]—dc22   2004050254

ISBN 978-0-7636-3416-2 (paperback)
ISBN 978-1-5362-0882-5 (reformatted paperback)

19 20 21 22 23 24 TRC 10 9 8 7 6 5 4 3 2 1

Printed in Eagan, MN, U.S.A.

This book was typeset in Goudy.

Candlewick Press
99 Dover Street
Somerville, Massachusetts 02144

visit us at www.candlewick.com

For my mother, Virginia,
roaming wolf country

Every thing possible to be believ'd is an image of truth.

WILLIAM BLAKE

The animal woke before dawn. Its body was curled tight against the frost that spiked the foot of the mountain, and except for the deep eyes that blinked and closed and blinked again, the creature made no move, as if the cold had frozen it through. It lay in a shallow pocket of rock, and the parts of its body that touched the mountain were warmer than those parts exposed to the wet morning air. In time, a shiver ran along its muscles, and it rumpled itself into a tenser ball. Its coat was thick but short and did not seem an adequate covering to see the animal through these chilly resting hours, yet every dawn it woke again, blinking and yawning, and the breath billowing out between its great wide jaws would take form and swirl, an echo like a memory of the animal itself.

A black-winged pewee arched across the clearing, so low to the ground that its white breast feathers disturbed the tips of the grass. It saw the animal in time to alter its course sharply, jerking into the sky as if caught on the end of a string, its wings folding under its belly and flashing into a spire above its head. The animal's eyes were closed, but it opened them when the bird chattered in rage and alarm, the tiny body ducking up and down, a flurry of black and white and noise. The animal considered the bird momentarily, its ears swiveling a reluctant degree. The bird rushed forward and immediately backward, seeing its reflection skim the animal's eyes. It changed direction without effort, as though turning itself inside out, and shot away into the trees. The animal watched it perch and plump and launch again, and in a second it was gone. Awake now, the creature scanned the branches, the rocks, the tangled random smatterings of scrub. Its damp nose angled, detecting everything and nothing. The short whiskers that lay flat along its muzzle flexed as it stretched open its mouth suddenly; the tongue curled between the canines and lazily swiped the nose. Then the animal settled its chin into the nook between its ribs and thigh and closed its eyes once more.

As on every other day now, he woke up at dawn. One moment he was sleeping and the next he was awake, and nothing had disturbed him to cause the difference but he was awake and alert as if an alarm had rung or he'd felt some knifelike pain. It seemed to him that sleep and wake were extreme things that should ease gently into each other, but that was never how it was for him. He was awake; his eyes were open; he knew where he was and who he was and what he had to do that day. He lay in bed only minutes before swinging his feet from under the bedclothes and placing first one, then the other, on the floor; he pushed back the blankets that pressed about his shoulders and sat up, wiping the night from his face with the heel of a hand. He took his dressing gown from its hook and slipped his arms through the sleeves as he padded down the hall, and he was in the kitchen coaxing a flame in the fireplace before the shape of his head had smoothed away from his pillow. Mornings were like this even on days when he woke knowing he had nothing to do: he was up and active and ignoring the cold. Usually his dog would be beside him, a golden-eyed familiar overseeing his every move, but this morning Moke was not around, and when he whistled, she did not come. Everything he did was geared to silence, and his whistling was soft, but if she was anywhere in the house, she would have heard, and come.

He filled the kettle high so he had time to dress before it boiled, sliding his cold legs into colder jeans and his feet into boots of hard, scuffed leather, and when he had made the tea, he took his mug outside, to see the day and to look for Moke. The night had been frosty, but the ice was melting under the sunrise, leaving the yard glistening and drenched. A row of sheds and stables enclosed the garden and the orchard and blocked his view of what lay beyond, but he knew. He knew that if he skirted the empty stables and the pock-marked swaying sheds, he would see land, land that could be called nothing more than that because there was nothing more to it. It was not flat land—it rose and fell into halfhearted humps and gullies—and apart from the occasional stand of evergreens, it was empty land, infested with a tough silvery grass that grew as high as his kneecaps and could shear skin from a finger with its edges, could puncture flesh with its points. Sometimes the wind barreled across the land like a hurricane and flattened completely the grass on the crest of each lolling, weak-willed hill, and the sight of this would fill him with a kind of smirking glee, like a child who sees its brother make short work of a bully.

The land beyond the rust-riddled sheds was a dirty brown, silver shimmering desert: what grew on it needed no water, and what water fell on it soaked only deep enough to turn the topsoil into slime. If you were lost in this place, you would die as surely as if you were lost in a desert of sand.

He tipped the tea leaves on the garden and went inside for the car keys, expecting to see Moke standing on the linoleum with her tail wagging sheepishly, but the kitchen was as empty as before. He set the guard before the fireplace, collected the keys, and went out again, detouring to the chicken run and scooping a tinful of grain from the barrel. The hens were waiting for him, clustered close to the wire, silenced by anticipation. He muttered words to them, but their round bright eyes watched the tin in his hands, and when a single brown grain fell to the ground, they squabbled against the wire, stretching their necks to reach it. He smiled: he liked the way they were so thoroughly self-absorbed. He, or a shape like his, would enter their thoughts at dawn, and they would watch for his appearance like fanatics promised a visitation—then he would feed them, and they would instantly forget him. He swung his arm, and the grain swept into the air and over the fencing, raining down on heads and sloping backs.

The station wagon was cold, and the sound of the engine struggling was harsh and loud and seemed to rattle the surrounds like marbles in a drum. He let the motor idle longer than it needed, and cast a glance guiltily at his father's bedroom window, but Moke did not come bounding to the seat beside him and eventually he released the brake. He let the wagon coast down the driveway, and when it reached the road, he pressed the accelerator and turned the car uphill, toward the shagginess of the mountain.

The sun rose around the sleeping animal and pricked out the color in its coat, the sooty tip of each dun-brown hair, the rim of whiteness on the brink of each neat ear. The frost vanished quickly once the thaw had begun, sliding down the gutters of the grass to form a ball of water that soon seeped into the dirt. Birds came down in their hundreds and strutted across the balding earth, wattlebirds and soldier birds and wagtails and crows, the biggest watching the smallest and striding in to snatch what those smaller eyes found.

The animal, too, was a thief and an opportunist. If given the chance, it would take a duck or a lamb, loping through a farmyard on its large, sure-placed paws. But most often it stayed true to its nature, a wild thing hunting wild things, its success grounded not in quickness but in a tremendous slow patience. It was not fast, but it could track its prey for hours, and this capacity for endurance was as fatal as its jaws.

Something moved, and the breeze caught the scent of it as sure as it catches a feather, lifting it, carrying it. An opportunist, the animal flashed open its eyes.

The mountain always looked to him like the handiwork of something suffering and enraged — an earthbound god or monster with a broken heart it hated to have, punching its fist into the rocky orb that caged it. But the mountain was, in truth, a volcano, standing massively alone, so long inactive and so fiercely weathered that its once-angular summit had been blunted like a nib. The years had chiseled the mountain a different shape, and if its slopes had once been tidily conical, it now had a thousand different peaks and plateaus and boulders that clung perilously to its countless blackened sides, casting shadows where dirt could gather and wildflowers grow. It had no crater, having suffocated itself with lava until the cavern had filled in and closed over like a wound. On its flattened top and all over its sides, it jarred without reason in and out of itself, and it cried, too: water ran constantly down slick gutters on its hide, and great towers of moss grew in the path of this wetness and linked the earth greenly to the sky. Parts of its bulk had been tamed, signposts hammered into fissures and walking tracks painted on its scarred ancient rump, but much of the mountain's knuckled mass was unconquered, picturesque and treacherous, and people came not to walk it but to scatter ashes at its base. He had seen the mountain so often that sometimes he would forget to see it, but at other times he would be awed by it, amazed by the way it rose so colossal and badtempered out of the thin bleached countryside around it. And at other times, he would think of it as a gate that never opened to reveal what lay beyond, a barrier that forced him to turn back toward the ceaseless land.

When the track ended abruptly, he left the wagon and continued on foot along a surging, slippery path, the little chain saw he carried bumping regularly against his thigh. The breeze had lost the edge of its burning coldness, and his breath had stopped coming out as fog; the sky was white with morning haze, but the day itself would be fine. When he reached the clearing he put down the chain saw and took off the coat that bunched in folds around his wrists, slinging it safely in the crook of a tree. He had come to the wild side of the volcano, where there was a graveyard of trees, red-gum trunks and heavy branches that had cracked in the summer warmth or shattered with the winter chill. Here too were the victims of fires swept through in previous years, trees in random pieces with charry chewed outlines. The frost had left the wood moist and spongy, but beneath the bark would be a dry heart where slaters would be curled like raindrops and crumbs would mark the paths of borers. It would take an hour or more to cut the wood into wedges and stack it in the wagon, and it would be lonely work: he was sorry he had not waited longer, called louder, for his dog.

He set the chain saw against the cutting stump and pulled its starter cord: the tiny machine rumbled, and the cord went rattling to its housing. The engine gagged and stopped. He yanked the cord again, and the engine bucked and fell mute. Again, and the sound was like the peculiar cry of some mythical beast, a loud brittle yowl that was there and gone, the beast instantly slain. He shook the chain saw and heard the petrol slosh inside it. He tried the cord once more and this time the engine did not even sigh.

He took his hands from the machine and pondered it. He touched a finger to its set of hooked teeth. It was not his way to fly into a fury, to clench his fists or shout in frustration and slam the saw to the ground. Instead he strode to the battered wagon, the grass catching at him as he went and the mud suctioning his heels, and searched the car for an ax he knew was not there. He tramped back to the chain saw and tried the cord hopefully. The silence stayed everywhere, and there was grease under his nails. He gazed at the more portable branches on the ground, gauging if there were enough of them to salvage something for his effort.

Movement flickered on the edge of his vision, and he turned to locate it. A wallaby launched itself through the clearing, its pace even and unhurried, its chunky gray body sprung on two narrow, pointed legs. It came quite close to him and looked at him as it did so, the boat-shaped ears rotating in unison, but it did not quicken its pace and continued steadily on: it pushed through the vegetation and disappeared, the grass sweeping back together like curtains at the end of a scene.

He lifted the chain saw and a big twisting branch and carried both to the wagon. He traced his steps and collected three more branches, and the dampness of them soaked through his sleeves as he took them to the car, the muck they had been sunk in smeared his boots and jeans. A spotted slug clung to his wrist, and he flicked it away as he headed once more for the clearing. He carted another load, and by now his shirt was grubby and wet and his journeys back and forth were marked out in the grass and broken fernery, his feet sliding in overturned wads of leaves. He stopped to push the hair from his eyes and glanced at the car, at the vast space inside it that he was meant to fill. He sniffed and sat down on the cutting stump. The breeze was blowing in his face, and the haze in the sky had burned away. The birds that had been here when he arrived were gone, offended by the sight of him. The clearing was quiet enough for him to hear a falling leaf collide with the trunk that had supported it before hitting the ground softly, skidding a moment along a slant of buried rock.

The animal trotted into the clearing, its head low, its shoulders jutting and vanishing with each footstep. It stood tall enough to see above the grass, but it veered around the blades when it could, plunging over the spikes in elegant leaps when it could not find bare earth. He stared at it, and quite suddenly, it saw him: it paused, one foreleg lifted, and jerked its head in his direction. He squinted back at it, the sun bright in his eyes.

"Hey," he said. "Hey, dog."

It didn't move, not even lowering the raised leg. It was a handsome, tawny-colored creature, sinewy but not thin, larger than his own dog but not by much. Its eyes were a strange triangular shape, set in muted patches of white. On its back and over its flanks were distinct black markings, like shivers running down its spine. He knew all the dogs that lived in the surrounding country, but he had never seen this dog before, and he wondered if it had strayed, turned feral, become dangerous.

"You want that wallaby?" he asked. "It went that way."

He lifted an arm and pointed, and the animal swerved into the bracken, its smooth long tail slipping away. He listened a minute for any sign of it, but it was gone utterly as soon as it was gone from sight. He wondered what its name had been, who had owned it, what hard history had left it alone here, at the feet of the hanging volcano.

He made four more trips from the wagon to the clearing, and then there was no more wood he could carry without help, so he cleaned his hands on the rough surface of the chopping stump and drove back to town.

———————

Jessica Piper was standing in her front yard and danced a few steps at the sight of his car. She planted some fingers in her mouth and watched him walk across the lawn. "Pretty," he said when he reached her. She touched a hand to the ribbon in her hair and smiled remotely. "Is Leroy awake?" he asked.

She spoke around her fingers. "Yeth."

"Is he inside?"

She nodded, a solemn child.

"Can I go in?"

She removed her fingers and said, "Satch."

He looked at her, and she gazed up at him.

"Satchel oh wry," she said, and nothing more. She stood, swaying slightly, the ruby ribbons garish against her plain, pale face. She was six, an oversight in her family and frequently forgotten, and he wondered who had stirred themselves sufficiently to fancy up her hair. Her dress was creased and not warm enough for such a cold morning. He smiled at her and followed the path to the door, scuffing his boots clean on the mat.

Leroy was in his bedroom, and there was a suitcase flipped open on his bed. His younger brother Miles, with whom he shared the room, was sitting crosslegged on his own bed, and they both gave Satchel a cursory glance. "Hey," he said.

"Three hours," Miles said cheerfully. "Only three more hours."

"Shut up."

Miles paid his brother no attention. "Three more hours and this whole room is mine. Mine."

"So what?" spat Leroy. "You think I won't have my own room where I'm going?"

"Mine, mine," sang Miles. Leroy snarled at him, and then at Satchel. "How you doing," he said gruffly.

"You packed?"

Leroy shrugged: the things in the suitcase were jumbled and spilling from the sides, and Satchel knew he would get to the city to find he'd left everything behind. And that perhaps he would not care.

"Take all your junk," said Miles. "I don't want any of your stuff in my room."

"Get out!" Leroy barked. Miles widened his eyes; he hesitated, but another glance at his brother was enough to decide him and he climbed from the bed willingly, as though he went because he wanted to.

"No tears," he said in the doorway. "No hugging and crying, you two. We've all got to be brave."

Leroy stepped toward him, and Miles vanished in a blink. Satchel looked at Leroy, who flopped into the only chair and blew air through his teeth. "I can't wait to get out of here," he said. "I can't wait."

"You don't have to wait much longer."

"I still reckon you should come with me."

Satchel smiled, and leaned against the door. From somewhere in the house came wailing, as one Piper child tormented another.

"Think about it," continued Leroy. "We'd have a great time. You and me. We'd rent a place and I could help you find some work."

They were words he'd used before, the few words remaining of what had been a grander plan, and Leroy's voice held no real hope or enthusiasm. "You'll have a good time by yourself," said Satchel. "You don't need me there."

"I know that." Leroy still had the energy to be offended by this reply. "I mean—you should get out of here."

"I will."

"Yeah, you will, but when?"

"One day. Soon."

"Soon." Leroy hissed the word over his lip. "Don't let them keep you here forever, O'Rye."

This was a new tactic, and Satchel shifted his footing. "I'm not. They don't keep me here. Anyway, I don't mind it as much as you."

Leroy gazed at him without blinking, but let the matter go. "I'll send you a postcard," he said. "When I'm set up, you come and visit me."

Something was pushed over, a small table or a chair, and they heard Mrs. Piper's husky asthmatic shouting, the sound of a hand smacking flesh, a chorus of raised angry voices. Satchel and Leroy glanced toward the sound and then they looked at each other. "Three more hours," sighed Leroy.

"I'll come to the station and see you off."

"No—don't. I think Mum wants it to be just her and Dad and the kids."

"Oh."

"No offense."

"No."

"I mean, you're like family, but still. You know—mothers—"

"It doesn't matter," said Satchel. "I've got things I'm supposed to do."

Leroy nodded. He glanced at the suitcase and

back at his friend. "I'll send you a postcard," he repeated.

Satchel straightened, his cold shirt touching his skin. "Well," he said, "I'll get out of your way."

Leroy stood up quickly. "Look after yourself, Satch," he said. "Don't forget me."

It seemed to Satchel a strange thing to say: they had known one another all their lives, for over twenty years. "No," he answered, "I won't."

"Drop in and visit Mum sometimes. She'd like that. She likes you."

"All right."

They stood and stared shyly at each other, Leroy shorter than Satchel, more wiry and much fairer, the two of them like a cream cat beside a dark dog. "Say hello to your mum and dad," said Leroy, and then, "Oh, shit, that just reminded me."

He took from his desk a fold of dollars, a brand-new twenty and two wan fainted tens, and handed them to Satchel. "That's for the work your dad did on the washing machine. Mum asked me to give it to you."

"Don't worry about it—"

"No, no, take it—"

"You keep it, you'll need it later—"

"You need it now," Leroy said tersely. "Take it, Satch, don't be stupid."

So Satchel took the notes, and put them in his

pocket. They glanced once more at each other, and Leroy said, "Well, I'll see you around."

They shook hands and smiled awkwardly, and Satchel said, "Take care, Lee."

Leroy did not follow him from the house. Jessica was still standing aimlessly in the garden, in almost the same spot. She turned her head to watch him get into his car but she did not move when he lifted a hand to wave goodbye.

Moke pushed past the fly-screen door and flew at him, the slashing of her fringed tail swinging her whole body into spirals. Her circular golden eyes were fixed on him as she leapt again and again to get close to his face. She was a crossbred creature with a shaggy red-fox coat and four feathery white paws, but she was so clever and he knew her so well that he hardly ever thought of her as an animal, and when she did something peculiar to dogs he could be surprised, and slightly disappointed. Five years ago his mother had given Moke to Satchel as a present on his eighteenth birthday, a red squirming puppy that she'd bought from a farmer and brought home on the seat of her car. The O'Rye family had never kept pets, and at the time it had seemed a bleak judgment on their future, that his mother should think he was in need of a dog.

Moke followed him into the kitchen, where Satchel's

17

father was sitting at the table with the newspaper flat out in front of him and his nose hovering close to the words. William's eyesight was fading, but he would not concede he needed glasses. He lifted his head as his son crossed the room to hang his coat on its peg: he had blue crescent eyes in a broad kindly face, and his black hair spiked out from his skull in a way that reminded Satchel of how the grass grew from the ground. "Cup of tea?" he asked, and, "Why are you so dirty?"

Satchel sat as his father stood. "The chain saw is broken."

"Broken?"

"I couldn't get it to work."

William picked up the kitchen clock and brought it close to his face. "I won't have time to fix it today."

"Why not? What are you doing?"

"Things," his father answered evasively. "Lots of things."

"There's a stack of timber in the back of the wagon. It has to be cut up."

His father turned to him, grinning brilliantly, his blue eyes twinkling. "You brought home logs?" he chirped. "Whole entire tree trunks?"

Satchel did not smile. "They need cutting, Dad."

William shrugged and turned his attention to the teapot. Satchel slumped on his elbows. On the table were signs that, in his absence, his mother had returned from work and had some breakfast before going to bed for a few hours. Satchel sighed, and looked down at his dog. "Where was Moke this morning?" he asked. "I couldn't find her. Was she locked in your room?"

"Moke and I went out for a walk. A brisk long walk."

"At six in the morning?"

"Earlier than that. Around five, more like it. Mokey and me."

"I called her," said Satchel. "I looked for her. You should have told me you were taking her out."

"Why? Is it against the law now, to take the dog for a walk? Against Satchel O'Rye's law?"

Satchel said nothing. His father dropped the lid of the teapot and it clattered loudly in the sink. "Now see," he said crossly, "see what you made me do? You'll wake your mother, Satchel."

Satchel looked at his hands, at the grease grubbed under his nails. William had let the fire wane to orange coals and the air near the floor was tinged with coolness. "Please try to look at the chain saw, Dad," he muttered. "Today. I need it fixed today."

"I'll see. I'll try. I'll try to find the time."

Satchel closed his eyes, felt relief from a weariness he didn't know he suffered. The sound of a car horn blaring made him open them again. Moke's ears shot upright, and she looked toward the door. William was pouring the tea, and he pretended he hadn't heard the sound. He set the cup before his son and resumed his seat. "Newspapers," he said lightly. "There's never anything new in them."

The horn sounded a second time, and Moke cast a glance at Satchel.

"The errors of mankind," said Satchel's father, "are repeated over and over. Always have been, always will. Look in your history books, you'll find the same old story. People never learn."

Satchel could hear the engine of the car idling. On the scarlet surface of his tea floated three small ant-like leaves.

"There's nothing new under the sun," stated William. "What we need is a new sun, perhaps."

The car horn flared again and Satchel said, "It'll wake Mum."

His father was suddenly galvanized: he reared from his chair and marched through the house to the front door. Satchel took his cup and followed him, Moke scrambling at his heels. His father had crossed the veranda and was stopped in the center of the stained concrete yard by the time his son caught up with him. There was a long, low-set car stretched between the petrol pumps. "What do you want?" William called to its occupants.

"Petrol," said the passenger. He'd lowered his window

just slightly, keeping the chilliness out. The window was tinted, and only his eyes could be clearly seen.

"We're closed."

The passenger leaned to the driver, and they exchanged some words Satchel could not hear. The passenger's eyes appeared at the window once more.

"You don't have to open the place," he said. "All we need is petrol."

"No," said William.

The passenger's eyes ducked away as he consulted the driver. Satchel sipped his tea. The petrol pumps had ceased working long ago, their underground supply tanks ringing hollow. The rickety building that had once been the office had junk scattered on its shelving and a cash register whose drawer was a nursery for spiders; its glass doors were linked at the handles by a sturdy length of chain. The petrol station appeared, to Satchel, so stark and obviously derelict that he wondered what terrible place these travelers had come from that they could mistake the place for operational.

As he thought it, they seemed to realize it. The passenger's voice was raucous when he spoke again. "What can we get here, then?" he asked. "Can we get a Coke? Can we get air? You got any air?"

William rocked slightly, his weak gaze drifting. The passenger stared at him, and at Satchel, for a moment or two. "We need petrol," he insisted.

"Not here."

"Can you tell us where, then? Can you at least do that?"

His tone made Moke twitchy, and she took a taut step nearer the car. "Get back on the highway," Satchel told the travelers. "There's a service station not far from where you turned off. You'll make it there all right."

The passenger's eyes switched to him. "If you're going to have a petrol station," he said, "you should at least sell goddamned petrol."

William's lip jerked; he and his son watched the car pull away, spinning up splatters of clammy dirt from the earth that lined the road. "Maybe that's something I can do tomorrow," Satchel suggested. "I could pull down that old building. The office. People wouldn't stop here then, maybe."

"It's not the building's fault," William said curtly. He turned and went back to the house. Moke stayed by Satchel's side, staring along the road where the car had disappeared, her body braced against the lingering urge to bark. Satchel walked to the office and peered through its doors, at the racks of dusty shelving, at the counter behind which his father had once worked. It would only take a few hours to knock the whole thing down.

In the house he changed his clothes for overalls, his boots for a pair with steel in their toes. He shaved his face and brushed his teeth and hair. He took Leroy's money from his shirt pocket and trod quietly along the hall. His mother's door was closed, but he turned the knob and looked into the room. She lay bundled in the middle of the old double bed, the blankets hardly bothered by her size. Her son tiptoed across the room and placed the notes beneath the base of the bedside lamp. His mother opened her eyes and looked at him and he knew she was the one he got it from, the ability to wake and be aware of everything.

"Dad fixed the Pipers' washing machine," he whispered, his words coming out foggy because the bedroom was achingly cold, the air painful to breathe. "That's forty dollars there. I'm going to work, but I'll be home for dinner."

She tipped her head, a vague wonky nod. Satchel went to his own room to get another blanket, and when he returned to drape it over her, she had gone back to sleep. He closed her door behind him and wished he could lock it — not lock her in, but lock other things out.

William was sitting in the same kitchen chair, studying the same page of the paper. Satchel took wood from the box and arranged the pieces in the fireplace, prodding the coals around them. William watched from the corners of his eyes. When he spoke, his voice was full of the spleen that the scene outside had brewed in him. "Where are you going?" he asked.

"You know."

"Speak politely to your father, Satchel."

"I'm going to help Gosling."

William's mouth curled. Satchel knew he would have an opinion and knew what it would be, so he didn't wait to hear it: he caught for his coat and snapped his fingers for his dog. He didn't stop to unload the branches and stack them beside the house, but climbed into the car and pumped the accelerator hard and hopefully. For once the wagon started without argument and he was grateful, and as he drove through the town and slung the car onto the highway, he felt refreshed and revived, as if his day had finally begun, and would get better from now.

The animal lay flopped in its rocky hollow, its eyes reduced to black slivers in the smudging of white. It would not wake for the rest of the day, not even when the birds were at their most piercing and the trees shook with their weight. It had tracked the wallaby with saintly patience, tapping every instinct intently. Once or twice it had dropped to its haunches, hardly touching itself to the earth, and was up again in an instant, resuming its measured trot. For some time the wallaby had not realized it was being shadowed, but when it did so, it had veered away from the foot of the mountain, away from the obstacles of rocks and trees and from the

24

shelterless hunting ground that was the volcano itself. It had made for barren country, trusting in its speed and the tangle of grasses to eventually deter its pursuer from the chase. The animal, knowing its quarry, had also known the likelihood of the tactic. Well into the morning it had kept up its pace, always out of reach of the keen marsupial eyes, always just on the periphery of the still keener ears. The wallaby could not outrun its hunter, for the animal would not race; the wallaby could not rest a moment, because the animal did not stop. It panicked when it understood this, and its fear made it dash erratically: it went close to the highway and the animal trotted for a distance on the edge of this open, perilous path. It swerved into cover when it felt a vibration through the pitch and found the wallaby frozen there, resigned.

So the animal slept for the remainder of the day, undisturbed by flies that landed on its paws, deaf to the daytime sounds.

The highway always reminded him of something young and harebrained, something aware of its size but not of its strength: it was like a colt bucking around a paddock, flash and damaging. He could still remember a time when the highway didn't exist, and the raised harried voices that had greeted the plans for its creation. His town lay bunched against a road that led to a larger town, but the highway was designed to bypass his town, and a hundred small towns like it, completely. Instead, it whipped straight from the city to the big town and on to other big towns, cutting off the little towns from the flow of the traffic as if little towns insulted it and it only had eyes for things as indelicate as itself. The road that curved through his town was now referred to as the Old Road, while the highway, laid a decade past, was New.

And no one traveled the old, meandering, narrower road unless their car was faltering, or they needed the facilities in the public park, or they were deliberately taking in the sights and finding there was nothing to see.

His town had a name, a proper name that could be found on maps. But the people who lived there were sunk by the dislocation that the new road had caused, by the feeling that they and their town were no longer of any necessity: they lived on the old road now, and their town had no further need of a distinguishing name. In their words they used its true name, but in their thoughts they called it little. On maps it was the smallest speck that a place could be, a mark the size a pin would leave if its tip was dipped in ink.

The big town was twenty minutes' drive along the highway, a place churned up in the gold rush and with its feet sunk in gold ever since; it seemed to grow and grow, and Satchel worried that one day he would look from his bedroom window and see the approach of its chimneys and flags. While the little town grew gaunt, while businesses failed and families moved away, the big town had swelled on a diet of cars that had boomed down the highway without stops or divergence, on money that had not been sapped by the humble shops that clung to obstinate existence in minor settlements everywhere. The gardeners in the big town grew fuchsias, which they planted along their fence lines and tended with great care: these plants were not normal, but had a tall single stem and a mass of froth and greenery spurting from the top. To hem the plants to this strange, unnatural design, the gardeners regularly nipped off buds that sprouted on the length of the willowy stem. These fuchsias reminded Satchel of the highway, of the huge town it invested its might into feeding, of the fated little towns that had grown in the wrong place. His mother said it was the fashion for people to prune their plants this way, but Satchel wondered if they weren't growing some idol to the bitumen deity that sustained them, a celebration of their status as a chosen people.

It was to the big town that he'd come to learn to be a carpenter, catching the bus that coursed six times daily along the old road, taking farmers to the movies and teenagers to the department stores, taking Satchel to the school that taught him a trade. And it was to the big town he returned when there was work that let him use his skill, when Gosling would phone and say there was room enough for him on the crew, work for a month or a week or a day. Gosling had grown up in the little town, had been a brotherless boy when William had been a tolerant teenager who'd dropped spare change in the younger's hand, and now Gosling was pleased to sling Satchel a job whenever he could do so, when the other workers wouldn't object to the presence of a ring-in who needed the money.

The building was almost finished, and when Satchel arrived, he saw men crawling about on the unfleshed parts of its skeleton: the men had been at work since dawn and any observer would think they were working conscientiously, but they were not. Gosling had them on go-slow, stringing the job out as long as he could. The foreman wandered over as Satchel parked his car, and Moke jumped out the window to greet him, as though she understood that this was a man she should charm. Gosling was a wide, careful, painstakingly decent man, his brow much furrowed with the weight of his own world and those of others that he adopted as his own, but he made no comment about Satchel being late. The work could not be stalled for much longer without suspicion being aroused, and it seemed that now the entire concept annoyed him. "Cultural center," he snarled. "This place already has a tourist center and a history center and a bloody replica mining village, and now it wants a cultural center. What are they going to put in it? What have they got left to put in the thing?"

Satchel squared his hands on his hips, and together they considered the structure. Gosling knew what was going in it, and he'd previously had words to say about that, too. When it was finished, there would be a souvenir shop and a bush-tucker restaurant, but these things were to be secondary to a collection of Koori artifacts. Gosling had said, "The people who built this town booted out the Aborigines. Give us your land, they said, and get the hell out. Take your sticks and boomerangs with you. If you come back, we'll shoot you. All changed now, though. Now it's *Look at this, look at that, this is genuine and original, it'll be fifty dollars thanks*. Hypocrisy, that's what this is. Hypocrisy."

He said the word again now: "Hypocrisy."

He looked at Satchel, and blinked his lashy eyes. The foreman's eyes and eyelashes were a pretty, startlingly feminine feature in his otherwise lined, blokey face. "How's your pa?"

"The same as yesterday, Gos."

"And your mother?"

"She's fine."

Gosling nodded contemplatively, reassured of the normal state of things. He said, "They tell me they're going to plant native trees around this place when it's finished. Just like the ones they cut down years ago."

Satchel made a short effort of brooding over this irony. Then he asked, "Where do you want me to start, Gos?"

The foreman gave him instructions, and Moke rambled autonomously around the adjoining land while Satchel worked beside the roofers, stepping along timbers that dropped to nothingness on either side. He heard the train pass through the town's center and thought of Leroy and his haphazard luggage boarding it when it pulled into the station near Satchel's home, and knew that when he ate dinner that night, Leroy would be just arriving in the city, rumpled from the journey but brimming with the thrill. Some time after midday the builders paused for coffee and sandwiches and then worked languidly into the afternoon, while Moke slept in the shade of the wagon and Satchel rolled up his sleeves to absorb the milky warmth of the sun.

They ate in the dining room because William liked the evening meal to be formal, his wife at one end of the table and himself at the other with Satchel's seat midway between the two, the little family separated by expanses of oak that forced them to stretch to reach the pepper grinder. This was the best room in the house, and except when eating, they used it rarely, so Laura O'Rye kept in here the things she valued, which might be broken by regular contact, housing them in a glass cabinet. Here were angular glass animals and precious cups and saucers, a marriage certificate and Satchel's christening mug, a parade of porcelain figures and a framed etching of Laura as a girl. Here too was something that it always pained Satchel to see: a small plate propped on a plastic stand with the words *I Love My Mom* and a bouquet of pansies printed on the plate's yellowed surface. He remembered buying it as a child with money his father had given him and being so proud to present it to Laura for her birthday. He was pleased she still treasured it, but its ugliness appalled him, and as a teenager its bland sentimentality had embarrassed him before his friends. With Leroy gone, it occurred to him that there was no one left to laugh at it now.

As soon as William sat down, he said, "No, I didn't fix the chain saw, but I'll do it tomorrow."

"What did you do, then?"

"I have my projects. I attended to my projects."

Satchel's father, since abandoning the service station, had pursued an artistic career. He painted miniature watercolors, a magnifying glass hovering between his face and the bristles of the brush. His subject matter was exclusively religious, and he favored in particular imagined scenes from the childhood of Jesus. In William's imagination, Jesus's youth had been polluted with omens, and he was forever encountering a young, wicked, gambling Judas, or getting splinters in his palms. Hung above the cabinet was a series with which the artist was evidently especially pleased, for he had enclosed them in silver framing: the first depicted Jesus assisting Peter when the future pope had slipped over a rock, the next showed him handing a shiny coin to the beggarly waif Barabbas, and the last had the adolescent savior the only person who stood upright in a quivering crowd round Pontius Pilate. These miniatures, painted on thick expensive paper, mortified Satchel, for Jesus was always a replica of himself as a child, slender and blue-eyed beneath a mess of shaggy hair, and Mary resembled Laura, and Joseph, who featured frequently, was William O'Rye himself.

It was humiliating enough when William showed off his art to visitors; Satchel lived in fear that one day he would produce a set of Christmas cards, or donate a piece to the church.

William clasped his hands above his meal and his wife and son followed suit. "We thank you for what we are about to receive," he murmured, "though I've never greatly liked pasta."

"You've never complained before," said Laura.

"Complaining is not my way," said William.

His wife flicked up an eyebrow. Turning to Satchel she asked, "How was work?"

"Good. Gosling says the project is hypocritical."

William chortled. "But he doesn't mind building it, though. He doesn't mind taking money for it. You should think about that, Satchel."

"Gosling has four children to feed," Laura replied tartly. Satchel looked at his bowl, and he and his mother sat in suspense for a moment, but William let the comment go by. "When you go to town tomorrow," he told his son, "pick me up some sketching paper — you know the type I like."

The family applied itself to its spaghetti, and for some minutes the only sounds were those of rowdy sparrows roosting beyond the window and the clink of cutlery on porcelain.

"Leroy left today," said Satchel, and his parents looked at him. They knew about Leroy's going, and he wondered why he'd said anything.

"No doubt he'll get into as much mischief there as he did here, and it'll be worse than ever. Stupid of his mother, to let him go."

"It wasn't stupid at all, William. What was Leroy supposed to do? How else can he get a house, a car, some sort of security in his life? There's nothing here for a boy like him; there's no work and nothing for him to do. He can earn his living in the city, do what he's been trained to do. I think he's done the sensible thing."

Again, the ground she trod was precarious, but Laura seemed not to care. "If Satchel couldn't get any work," she added, "I'd expect him to do exactly the same."

William glanced at her sullenly, twirling his fork in his bowl. Laura turned to her son. "You'll miss Leroy," she said, "won't you?"

"I guess."

"Maybe, when he's settled, you should visit him for a week or two."

Satchel nodded. "Maybe."

"It's not good," said William, "when we're all here together, to talk about one of us leaving."

Laura gave him a steady look. "We'll talk about it when the time comes, then," she said.

William was fidgeting: the conversation had agitated him, as they all knew it would, and Laura waved Satchel's attention to his dinner. They ate quietly, William shaking more and more salt upon his food. Their conversations were often punctured by these long, stressful silences, the family letting cool an argument that a guest may not have even noticed. Satchel knew that his parents loved each other, and that they loved him, too, but it seemed to him that affection must be a weak kind of thing, piddling compared to apprehension.

Yet it was hard, sometimes, not to talk about working, when work was all Satchel and his mother did. They could not even talk about Moke, because the dog had spent the day at the building site and, if William was really as upset as he seemed, that slim connection would be enough.

So they talked about the weather, and the night's TV programming, and the chicken that had gone off the lay. Later, when William had left to take his bath and Laura and Satchel were clearing the table, Laura said, "I'm sorry, Satchel."

"It doesn't matter."

"My hands were hurting."

"Show me."

She turned up her palms and he came close to examine them. Laura was a nurse at the hospital in the big town, and in the past year her hands had started reacting to the pills she had to crush for the feeble patients. Now, everything seemed to make the problem worse — detergent in the washing water, the lotions she liked to buy. Gloves would make her skin sweat, and moisture made the condition blaze. The doctors had tried everything that might fix it, and it would not go away.

The flesh of her palms was cracked so deep that Satchel could see into depths of angry red. The skin around the cracks was heated and peeling and the flesh was vaguely swollen. Her hands looked so sore and abused that he winced, feeling a sick kind of heartache. "Mum," he said, "you can't live like this. You have to quit."

She scoffed bravely, as he had known she would. He was much taller than his mother, and he looked down at her desperately. She seemed so small, smaller than she'd ever been. Her hair was dyed because she did not want it being drab and gray. She always dressed as well as she could, and the stubbornly jaunty daisies knitted into her jumper filled him with a wretched grief. He hated it that she had to do the grim heavy work of a hospital, hated that she had to work all night because it paid more, and he hated that she shouldn't be allowed to rest now, when she was getting older and so much of her life had been difficult.

"They're never going to get better," he said softly, "unless you leave the hospital."

Laura pulled her hands away and turned back to the table. "Go and check that your father hasn't drowned," she said, impatient with him now. Instead he went and washed the dishes, running the hot tank empty so William could not refill his bath.

Later, when he was curled up in bed reading and he thought she had gone to bed, she came into his room in her dressing gown and set some money on his desk. He asked, "What's that for?"

"For the paper William wants."

"If he wants paper for his drawings he should pay for it himself."

"Satchel," she sighed. He gazed at her bleakly, but she smiled at him. "It's the money from the Pipers, for him fixing their machine. So he is paying for it himself, really."

He folded the book and dropped it to the floor; his mother wished him a good night. When she'd left the room and he'd turned off the lamp, Moke came creeping out from beneath the bed and jumped up to sleep beside him.

On Sunday they went to church together, Satchel going because it was easier to go than refuse. They had to drive all the way to the big town because the priest only came to the little town on the last Sunday of every month. When he did so, the pews of the tiny wooden church would be crowded, and people would stand along the walls; Satchel could look around and recognize every face, and hear the thoughts behind them. He knew who was dying and who did time in purgatory, who needed a miracle and who had not been seen or heard from in years. Above and below these was the common prayer, the unanswered, eternal prayer: the one that asked for rain, for real, drenching rain in place of moldering drizzle. But the church in the big town was a huge construction, built in stone and paid for with gold. It was very cold inside it and half its seats were empty, and Satchel could hear nothing except the monotony of the priest. He sat beside his mother and looked up at the vaulted ceiling: he counted seven pairs of buttresses supporting its great length. The windows were wide and dazzling, and through the colored glass he could see the shadow of protective wire. He didn't listen to a word the priest said, and cast a startled glance at the altar only when a jangle of bells sounded as the priest raised the host to the sky.

He wondered what Leroy was doing. On Saturday night they had often caught a lift to the big town and gone to one of the many hotels. At the end of the night they would try to find someone with a car that was going their way, and failing that they'd hitchhike, and more than once they had walked the entire distance home. Last night Satchel had sat in the lounge room watching television, fighting off the feeling that this was how he would spend the rest of his life.

A hymn began and he reached for the song book, looking at his mother's copy to see what page he should be on. He glimpsed the raw flesh of her hands as he did so, the deep bloodless cracks that had opened in the creases of her palms, the red slivers at the base of these cracks. He closed his eyes and asked a God he didn't believe in to cure his mother's hands. She needed her hands, and he needed her hands to be better. *Please*, he prayed, *I never ask you for anything.*

The wounds in Laura's palms reminded him of something, and for a time he couldn't recall what it was. The cracks in her flesh and the redness underneath resembled a creature splitting its skin in order to step from it as something changed. His mother would emerge red all over, as if she'd been terribly burned. And then he remembered the dog he had seen at the mountain, with its back and its flanks lashed with stripes. It, too, had looked this way: it looked like the animal had grown a black coat beneath its fawn hide and that it would soon step forth unrecognizable. Its new jet color would disguise it, and show that it was wild.

He heard William's impatient mutter and opened his eyes to find his parents staring at him and the rest of the pew empty. He scrambled into the aisle, and as the queue edged forward for Communion, he could hear his mother humming the hymn behind him, and William's flat, hesitant attempts to sing.

But on the way home, William surprised them by saying, "I don't believe I agree with everything that priest said today. I don't think we should be unquestionably forgiving. There's plenty of things that don't deserve forgiveness."

Laura glanced in the rearview mirror, and Satchel in the back seat caught her look. If William sang, it usually meant he was happy, but now it seemed they couldn't even rely on that. "Breach for breach," said

William, gazing through the window at the speeding scenery, "eye for eye, tooth for tooth: as he hath caused a blemish in a man, so shall it be done to him."

"Revenge is *mine*, says the Lord. Not yours, Dad."

"Fools despise wisdom and instruction, Satchel. Surely you see there is a difference between taking revenge and refusing to forgive."

"I see it. But isn't there something about turning the other cheek?"

William sighed, patiently. "If someone were to murder you, Satchel, and chop you into little pieces, and leave the pieces floating in a drain, would you want me to forgive that someone?"

"I don't suppose it matters what I want, Dad. You're the one who's always doing what you say God has told you to do."

"Satchel," said Laura, "be quiet."

He slumped against the door and stared petulantly at the back of his father's tufted head; William, too, went silent, but Satchel knew he wasn't pondering any inconsistency in his creed. He had a stockpile of biblical quotations he could rattle out like ammunition, but he was finicky, a connoisseur: only certain, trusted references would pass his lips, and he uppishly spurned all others, as if they originated from a different, less credible source. When countered with something that didn't suit him, he simply shut his ears.

41

Still, Satchel had reason to smile. When William disagreed with a sermon, the conflict always ran deeply and the O'Ryes would not, as a result, be seen in church for a while.

He walked with Moke along the railway track, past fenced-off scrubby paddocks bare of stock or crops. The district called itself horse country, yet it was rare to see anything fancier than a thick-necked pony or a nag in the shade of an evergreen. Few people farmed sheep here, and no one bothered with cattle. The stock corrals and loading ramps were empty, and weeds grew high around them. The dams were overflowing with a flat livid water that was sipped and sieved by egrets and gave the ducks a place to bathe. The farmhouses were set well back on the land and obscured by the hills; Satchel saw glimpses of roofs and threads of smoke from chimneys, but no windows or front doors. The train line was planted with bottlebrush and rice flower and they had to weave their way through it, Satchel taking his hands from his pockets unwillingly to push the strappy branches aside. A farm dog rushed them from behind, its approach unheard and surprising, making Moke yelp and spin. Satchel shouted and the animal retreated cringingly.

They took an unsealed side road that brought them back to town, passing the cemetery and the dilapidated flour mills, past a clutch of motley houses and the sign that welcomed travelers here and hoped they were driving safely. Of the dozen stores that lined the edge of the old road, seven stood sour and abandoned. The bank had closed, as had the doctor's and the real-estate agent's. There was a gift shop, which had tried to sell the townspeople their own craftwork — painted flowerpots and embroidered doilies, knitted teddy bears and leather-bound visitors' books — and there was a notice on its door saying that it, too, would soon close. But there was a tearoom with gingham curtains, and there was a bakery. There was a hairdresser with posters in its window showing grinning, gormless models, their eyes bleached white by the sun, sporting styles the hairdresser could never replicate. There was a fruit seller who managed to survive the many roadside stalls set up along the highway. There was a meeting hall with a clock in its weatherboard tower, where now and then old movies were shown. And, dead center of town, there were two hotels that stood facing each other from opposite sides of the road, the brows of their second-story verandas frowning in competition. No one was walking the footpath on this cold afternoon, and everything except Timothy's Take-Away was shut for the day.

Timothy was behind the counter, his head like an enormous shrike's egg, just as domed and flecked and bald. He was forever cleaning, and was inflicting his energy on the milkshake-maker when Satchel walked in with Moke at his side. Timothy's mouth turned down at the dog and Satchel told her, "Out."

"Regulations," said Timothy.

Satchel couldn't imagine a health inspector dedicated enough to come all the way out here, but he had no desire to torment the shopkeeper, who called and chaired innumerable ill-attended town meetings and seemed to think it his sole responsibility to keep the township functioning. Moke went and stood on the footpath, staring dolefully through the door; after some minutes she wandered away.

He asked for a hamburger and Timothy carefully recorded the order on his notepad. Satchel turned to take a seat at the table and found Chelsea Piper sitting there with a milkshake, her magnified eyes watching him. "Chelsea," he said, "hello."

She plucked the straw from between her lips and said, "You can sit here, if you like."

There was nowhere else, so he pulled out the chair and sat opposite her. The bubbles in the milkshake were popping rapidly, revealing the milk's level and the parsimoniousness of Timothy. She sniffed at the sight, and looked up at him. Her eyes, behind her glasses, were huge and startling, stained a flat stony gray. "Have you heard from Leroy?" he asked, for she evidently had nothing to say.

"He's staying with our aunty. He hasn't got a job yet. He's looking for a place to live. He phoned yesterday."

Satchel nodded. He could hear, in the kitchen, the hiss of mince upon the grill. He spluttered, "There must be plenty of work for a pastry cook. In the city, I mean. He'll find something."

Chelsea said nothing; her gaze was in her milkshake, which she gave a spiritless stir. She had never been a talker, and Satchel knew she was particularly nervous around him. When William had lost his job driving the school bus, the person given the position was Chelsea, and she was perpetually racked with guilt by the fact.

But Chelsea Piper was a person who seemed doomed to shrink and quail: always aware she was the least endearing of the tribe of Piper children, she had long ago decided that in silence she would find sanctuary and that isolation could protect her from hurt. She had never allowed herself to forgive the blunders of her younger years, determined that the witnesses to her stupidity had neither forgotten nor forgiven. She was twenty-one now, but she was haunted by the teenage girl she had been, a spotty, short, and rather ugly girl who had longed for friendship and affection but fell, instead, into an abyss of ridicule.

Satchel and Chelsea had gone to the same high school, a school in the big town that charged nominal fees but required its students to wear a pallid uniform.

Pupils traveled to attend it from many miles away, and in winter, classes would finish early to let the children of farmers be home before dark. Chelsea was a couple of grades below Satchel and her brother Leroy, but nonetheless Satchel was not unaware of the event that had caused uproar on the day that crushed Chelsea utterly.

She had been identified as the school's outcast early, forced to eat her lunches alone and wait until there were no further choices before being grudgingly accepted into a team. She was the girl that other girls passed notes about, the one who made the boys snicker and whisper crude suggestions. Her attempts to join a circle were seen as a slander upon that circle, and she was chased away like something infected. Desperate for acceptance and noting that the favored girls were often given nicknames, she once asked her mother to embroider the word *Chels* on the front of a windcheater, and she wore this to school on a free dress day. The word gained currency only as a term of mockery.

She'd weathered a year of *Chels* by the time she made her final, most monumental error. Satchel was in what would be his last months of schooling, and he could only imagine the suffering she endured in the remaining years she spent at the mercy of her classmates. At fourteen her interest was snagged on a noisy, popular, bovine boy who had never looked in her direction but to whom she began to devote every thought. Her mousiness, she decided, blinded him to her existence, and she concocted a plan that would lure his attention if only through the attention of others. It was an idea monstrous in its lack of subtlety, but she was young enough to think it would be greeted with amusement and admiration, that the bovine boy would find it enticing.

She trimmed his image from her class photograph and took the severed head to a shop in the big town that turned pictures into badges. She pinned the badge to her blazer and went, head high, to school.

It was a day that became legend. Satchel could remember Leroy with his hands pressed to his face, groaning with the anguish of his humiliation. And he could remember Chelsea sitting by herself on the long bus journey home, the badge removed from her blazer but two pinholes like puncture wounds showing in the lapel. He thought she would cry, but she never made a sound.

Now Chelsea herself drove a bus, a different bus for a different school, and the bovine boy had died when he rammed his car into a tree, and the people with whom she'd been at school had gone their different ways, some to places where they themselves were the ill-treated underclass. But Chelsea Piper never forgot the lesson that she was contemptible, and it seemed that she never would. She'd sucked herself in like a snail, inflicting herself on no one. She remained in the town as if chained to its road; he wondered if she stayed for fear of meeting someone, on a busy street somewhere, who had played a part in the torture that was that terrible day, and finding herself with nowhere familiar to run. Or if she stayed from a simple lack of desire to do anything anymore.

She was no easy person to talk to and he wished he had not sat down, for Timothy had ducked a glance through the fly-screen straps dangling in the kitchen doorway and seen him at the table. He wouldn't think to wrap the burger now, but would bring it out on a plate. Satchel watched Chelsea dip a finger in the foam that rimmed the milkshake container and blot clean the chocolate smear. He wondered if she found a peaceful pleasure in her exile: it would be nice, sometimes, to know that no one expected anything from you, no words, no thoughts, no cheerful greeting or enthusiasm. He scouted for a topic to break the stuffy silence: recalling that she liked animals and kept a horse in an agisted paddock, he asked her how it was. She said only, "Good."

Timothy dropped a utensil and spat out an irritable word. Chelsea skimmed the straw around the container raspily, keeping her enlarged eyes down. Finally she set the cup aside and dabbed her mouth on the sleeve of her jumper. She considered Satchel blankly and said, "I'm going to train him to barrel race."

"That'll be fun."

"He won't be any good at it. He's just lazy, that's why."

Timothy arrived with the burger. He put the plate on the table and said, "Five dollars, Satchel."

He stood close and wary-eyed while Satchel dug in his pocket and found the money, as if suspecting Satchel had plans for skipping town. He took the coins and stalked morosely back to his kitchen.

Chelsea made no move to leave, though she had nothing left to keep her in the store, and Satchel became conscious of her watching as he ate. By the third bite it seemed that his teeth were making an inordinately loud, distasteful noise; by the fifth he felt as if her gaze was stripping him naked. He put down the remains of the burger and cleared his throat. "Chelsea," he said, "have you ever seen a dog running around the mountain? A brown, striped sort of dog?"

"Joe Rinket has a brindle greyhound. It's brown, with blackish stripes."

"No, not a greyhound. Heavier set, more like a collie. It looked like a stray to me."

"Joe Rinket's greyhound isn't lost," she said. "I saw him with it this morning."

"You haven't heard anyone on the bus say their dog has disappeared?"

Chelsea shook her head, and Satchel felt sufficiently

composed to take the final bites. "If there's a stray dog on the mountain," she said, "someone will shoot it before long."

He nodded, cleaning crumbs off his plate.

"If there's one," she mused, "there's probably others."

He shook his head. "If there was a pack of feral dogs out there, we'd have heard about it. It was on its own, I think."

"When did you see it?"

"The other day—the day Leroy went away. I was getting wood. It cut across a clearing and stopped and stared at me. It was a strange-looking thing."

"Strange like how?"

It would be difficult to explain, so he went to the counter and searched behind it for a pen. He had inherited his father's minor artistic ability, and the animal he drew on a serviette looked right to him. Chelsea, however, glanced at it and laughed. "It's half a cat and half a dog," she said.

"But that's why it was strange. Its tail was like a cat's, and so were its ears and the shape of its face. But it had a muzzle like a dog, and it was the size of a dog."

"Maybe it was a cat. Feral cats are big."

"They don't have pointy muzzles, no matter how big they are."

Chelsea peered at the picture. She said, "You've drawn the legs too short, or the body too long."

"I've drawn it the way I remember it," he replied, a little testily. "Its body was a bit longer than its legs. And it had big, dark, triangle eyes."

"What are these squiggles?"

He took the serviette from her and sketched the stripes on the creature's back more distinctly. When he returned the drawing, she gazed at it for a minute, and then she looked around the shop, as if checking that Timothy was out of sight and they were still alone. She asked, "Where did you say you saw this thing?"

"At the mountain. Why? Do you recognize it?"

She didn't answer immediately: she tipped her head and her thick, lustreless hair bunched around her shoulders. "Maybe," she said. "Can I keep this picture, Satchel?"

"If you want it."

She tucked the serviette into her pocket and scanned the shop again. Moke was standing at the doorway and whined softly to catch her eye. "Your dog," she said. "She's tired of waiting for you."

Satchel said, "Yeah, I better go. I'll see you later, Chelsea. If Leroy rings, tell him I said hello."

He left his plate on the counter and went out to the street, forgetting Chelsea instantly to wonder, instead, where to go.

He walked with Moke toward the mountain because there was nowhere else that beckoned, no other element of the landscape that would overshadow him and let him feel alone. They followed the sealed road that was signposted for tourists and arrived at the picnic area with Moke panting and Satchel's sleeves pushed up on his arms. The three slat-pine tables were unoccupied and there was no one to be seen, but there were cars parked on the gravel and he could hear the sound of voices calling to each other from the flats well up the mountain. He tacked, with the dog, away from the mass of the volcano and into the spindly wilderness, where leaves and pipes of eucalypt bark and the airy shells of cicadas cracked to pieces under his feet. He wasn't going anywhere: he was simply keeping away. He didn't want to go home, knowing what his father's mood would be, a mood Satchel had pointlessly encouraged on the car journey home from church. He felt sorry for his mother and hoped that she, too, had slipped away from the house, but he guessed she had probably stayed. He might have stayed to help her but she preferred it if he took himself away. She didn't want him enduring what he could easily avoid. She wanted her son to feel none of the obligation that had so thoroughly hobbled her own life, and when he showed symptoms of doing so anyway, despite all her best teaching, she could become very angry at him.

Laura had met William at the wedding of some friends, and in his brightest moods William would marvel at the romance of it, two strangers who would spend their lives together meeting at the celebration of exactly such a destiny. Laura was doing her hospital training and William was the son of a farmer, but even then the signs were there that farming life would one day become difficult and William had come to the city to learn a trade that might support him: always a tinkerer, he was going to be a mechanic. They dated for four years, and during that time Laura worked as a surgery nurse while William qualified and found employment in a small suburban garage. William, at this time, was slightly less religious than his parents might have hoped he would be, and when Laura became pregnant, the couple had to hurry to marry. Laura laughed at Satchel's expression when she told him this story: "We were going to get married eventually," she said consolingly. "We didn't do it because of you." And Satchel believed her: the fact that they had loved each other was clear from the tales they told. But still, when he felt the weight of his responsibility, he knew it was pressing down on him from the distance of that careless day.

Satchel had not yet been born when William's widower father died and the family property was set adrift. William's brother didn't wish to run it, and neither did William himself. The land was parceled and sold to neighbors and the brother returned to his house on the coast. Laura, however, had listened to the stories the brothers told of their country boyhood, and she agreed with her husband that their own child would benefit from such an unfenced, healthy, barefoot upbringing. They need not be farmers, but they could use the money from a farm to buy a country business, and this they promptly did. They chose the service station in William's hometown, where as a kid William had bought puncture kits for his bicycle and where as a young man he had filled his first car with petrol. The town was five hours' drive from the city Laura had lived in all her life and, "Weren't you sad," Satchel asked his mother, "to leave your family and friends behind?"

"Oh yes, a bit," she conceded. "In the early days I was lonely. William already knew everyone, but I was a stranger. I was expecting a baby and I didn't know anything about babies: I missed my mother. For months, I rang her every day. But I suppose I would have gone anywhere with William. If he'd wanted to live on another continent, I suppose I would have gone."

The petrol station, its little store, and its big double garage were bringing in a reasonable amount of money then, and would do so for much longer to come — even years later, when the highway was laid but service stations had yet to be built along it, to the very day William closed the place down, it was making enough to keep them secure. The business came complete with the house and yard and the sheds behind it, and Laura worked to tame and make these buildings homely while William painted his name above the garage and introduced himself to suppliers. She began to make friends when the sheen of her newness rubbed off a little, and she earned respect the day she took a choking child by the heels and smacked it stoutly on the back, ejecting a slimy coin across the room. She called herself a farmer's wife, though William grew calluses and harvested engine parts, and in time she lost all desire to return to the shoulder-to-shoulder existence that was life in the city.

Satchel was born in September, in the evening of a cool, dry, windless day. His mother told him he had screwed up his eyes and howled at the sight of her and she had known from this that he would always be a father's boy. Later he would grow to look like William, with the same big bones and broad, friendly face, his eyes a color more purple than blue. He would dawdle about the garage while his father worked on cars and for his birthdays he unfailingly requested wrenches and motor-mowers. He seemed dazed the day it occurred to him that a child could have a brother or a sister: he asked his father why he had neither and William had replied, "I wondered that myself, Satchel. I reckon God thinks that people who are given a child like you are not allowed to have another, because that would be greedy."

And he had had a happy childhood: it had been long and safe and barefooted, a time he associated with the warbling of magpies and the sight of foxes in the field. It had been as carefree as Laura had hoped it would be. He grew up, and into, a country boy: he knew about traps and crops and drenching and guns, about the meaning of a pinky sky and about tending an orphaned lamb. He grew up an only child, skilled in amusing himself, the sole receiver of his parents' affection and aware that, one day, his parents would rely solely on him.

When he went home, much later in the afternoon, he asked his mother, "Where is he?"

"He's in his bedroom," said Laura, "painting. Stay away from him tonight."

He opened a can of dog food and scooped spoonfuls of it into Moke's dented dinner bowl. He took the meal outside to her, changed the water in her drinking tray, and hustled the chickens back to their coop. When he returned to the kitchen, he found his mother running water in the sink and said, "You know detergent is bad for your hands."

"Satchel," she said curtly, "what am I supposed to do? This house doesn't run itself. Someone has to do the dishes. Go and set the table, please. Don't worry about a plate for William."

That night he lay awake, his hands folded behind his head, and heard his father moving quietly through different parts of the house. After midnight, when William finally went to bed, Satchel climbed from under his blankets and walked around the house, switching off the lights in every room.

The animal stretched, and flashed its tongue around its nose. It stood straight and listened, its ears rotating and flexing to capture every sound. Naturally a nocturnal creature, it was well suited to the pitchness that engulfed it: its coat did not catch the moonlight, and its black eyes and nose absorbed any reflection. Slender and built for prowling, it maneuvered through the bracken on large, high-knuckled paws that touched the ground flat and soundlessly. Its sense of smell was remarkable, inundating it with information. It could detect its browsing prey, advance and dispatch it without giving the victim the chance to even realize it was there.

It heard the approach of another well before it saw it, but when the other raised its head above the grass and stared at it, the animal gave a short, hoarse yelp and bounded forward through the spikes. For a moment the twin animals spiraled, buffeting each other's shoulders, feet prancing on the earth. Then they veered and distance was between them immediately; but they trotted into the scrub, one following the other, and stayed near for the rest of the night.

Gosling called the crew together at lunchtime and told them what they already knew: that they could no longer string out the completion of the job and that there were approximately three more days of work to be done. Then, with the exception of one or two minor tasks, their part in the construction of the cultural center was over. The men looked into their sandwiches thoughtfully, giving the announcement due consideration. "No doubt, in a few months' time, they'll be asking us to build them a historical bathroom," said the foreman, but no one laughed, and Satchel chased off a fly that was buzzing in his face. Gosling looked somewhat stricken and walked rapidly away.

They were headed back to work, ditching the dregs

of last-minute cigarettes, when Gosling called him over. The foreman was sitting in the cab of his truck, sipping coffee from the mug of his flask. Moke wanted to climb in beside him and he shifted his knees to let her pass. "You want to come home with me?" he asked her. "You gorgeous little flirt."

Satchel crumpled his sandwich bag and waited while Gosling gave Moke's brow a rough patting. Finally the foreman looked at him and said, "Like I say, three more days, at the most, we're going to be here."

"Hmm."

"Have you got a job to go to after this?"

"No. Not yet, anyway. Something will come along."

Gosling laughed. "That's what I like about you, O'Rye. You never let circumstances get the better of you. You always keep up your hopes. You must have learnt that from your mother."

Satchel shifted his weight, squeezing the paper in his hand. Moke had clambered to the floor below the steering wheel and was dabbing crumbs off the dirty mat. Everyone knew about the problem of William but Gosling was one of the few who would speak out loud about it, however vaguely. Satchel didn't like it, but he owed Gosling these liberties. Now, the foreman turned somber and looked Satchel in the eye.

"I'll tell you this honestly," he said. "Nothing's going to be happening around here for the next six months or so. I've been putting a bit aside, and of course Mrs. Gosling has her job in the dress shop, so all the baby Goslings will survive. But I've been thinking about you. It's a long time to get through on your mother's paycheck. She's only working part-time, I hear?"

"She works night shift. It pays a bit better."

"Night shift." Gosling frowned and muttered to himself. "You ever done night shift, Satchel? It hurts you. Hurts your body and your brain. Still, when you need money, there's not much you won't do. Not when you've got yourself and a house and a husband and a grown-up son to support. I know you do your best not to be a burden, and I'm not saying you are one, but those are the facts. We all have to face facts. Not many people have it easy around here. Your family doesn't. You don't."

Satchel nodded. That people knew so much about the business of his family made him feel queasy, but there was nothing that wasn't known in a tiny town and nothing that didn't get spread around. The foreman ducked his head to see past Satchel, wagged a finger at the men dawdling around the building. "Half those blokes are in the same boat as you, O'Rye, if that's a consolation. They've tried their best all their lives, but it hasn't got them far. This time next week they'll be lying in bed wondering why they were born. And that's a bad thing, to wonder why you were born. To know it's always going to be a battle, always a bloody uphill struggle, and nothing's going to change."

Satchel sniffed, and nodded again. Gosling's eyes switched back to him and batted like butterflies.

"I've got a brother-in-law living up north," he continued. "Up where the beaches are. They've got coral reefs on their doorsteps there. Tom's got work for a good carpenter, and he'll take my word about someone who knows the trade and somebody who doesn't. He's got work that would keep a man busy for four or five months. Last time I was there he'd just bought a trailer, so you might get your accommodation thrown in with the deal — details like that could be decided at a later date. But it would be a nice situation, Satchel. Surf and sun and sand, and being your own boss. Getting away from here for a while. Seeing a bit of the world. Opening up your opportunities."

Satchel was studying the ground. "Yeah," he said faintly, "it sounds nice."

"There's nothing Tom wants done that you wouldn't be able to do. You're a good carpenter, better than you think. And I reckon he might even let you take Mokey, if you wanted to do that. Has Moke ever seen the beach?"

"No."

"She'd love it!" cawed Gosling. "You'd love it, wouldn't you, girl?"

61

Satchel lifted his eyes. Moke was trampling on the foreman's lap, her tongue darting all over his sweating face. "It's a kind offer, Gosling," he said. "I mean, it's good of you to think of me."

"You were the only person I thought of, O'Rye."

"I'm not sure how I'd get there . . ."

"We'll have that old station wagon spruced up and she'll make the distance, no worries."

Satchel smiled glumly. Gosling eased Moke away from himself and looked at Satchel. "Think about it over the next couple of weeks," he said, "and tell me what you decide."

"Yeah, I will. Thanks, Gosling. I mean—thanks."

"Yeah, I know what *thanks* means. Now get back to work."

Satchel trudged away, Moke rushing to join him, but he hadn't reached the shadow of the building when Gosling called him back again. The foreman was still sitting in the truck's cabin; he had refilled his mug with coffee.

"Listen," he told Satchel, "I'm serious about this. Don't you walk off and toss it out of your mind. I want you to give it some real consideration."

"I will, Gos."

"My arse, you will. I know you." He frowned at the dashboard and shook his head despondently. "Don't piss opportunity into the wind, Satchel. Don't kill yourself staying here, because no one's going to thank you for doing that. You've got a rough life here."

Satchel felt redness rising to his cheeks, and his gaze skimmed the ground. Gosling didn't speak for a moment; then he sighed through his teeth. "I don't mean to hassle you," he said. "You're not my kid, and you're a grown man. You know what you're doing, I guess. But promise me you'll think about it."

"I promise," said Satchel. "I will."

"It's not forever; it's just a few months. They'll be all right without you for four or five months."

"I promise," repeated Satchel, more firmly.

"Good," said Gosling. "Now get your hands out of your bloody pockets and get out of my sight."

Laura was taking clothes from the line when he arrived home, and he went out to the yard to help her. She glanced at her son from behind a pair of his trousers. "Good day?" she asked.

"Gosling says the building will be finished in a few days."

"Oh, well. That was always going to happen."

He unpegged a row of his father's faded flannels and dropped them in the basket. The clothes had been on the line all day but they were still damp and would need to be arranged on the guard before the fire. Until they were washed again, they would smell sweetly smoky. "What about you?" he said. "How's it been here?"

"Quiet. William painted for most of the day. Joseph is taking Jesus fishing."

Satchel snorted; even Laura was grinning. She seemed in a cheerful mood, and he asked her what had happened. "The Matron from St. Jude's rang," she explained. "One of their nurses has retired, and she asked if I wanted to take the position."

St. Jude's was a geriatric home in the big town, and Satchel asked, "What did you say?"

The breeze billowed a bed sheet into Laura's arms, and she swatted the cloth away. "I told her I'd think about it overnight. I suppose it's sensible to take it."

"But — an old people's home?"

Laura stooped, pressing pillowcases into the basket. "I can't stay at the hospital for the rest of my life. They've been cutting back the staff for a couple of years already. They won't give me extra hours, and they're always telling me I can't keep up with the new technology. I'll end up sacked if I don't leave soon. St. Jude's is probably my wisest choice. And I wouldn't have to do night shift there. It's morning and afternoon work."

The chickens were roaming the orchard, and Moke had started jogging around them, forcing them into a clutch of rolling eyes and flapping wings. Satchel called his dog away, ordering her to sit on the veranda. To his mother he said, "It would be horrible to work at a home, though. Depressing."

"Someone's got to look after the poor things. And anyway, it might be good for my hands. They mightn't use the same tablets there, and my hands will have a chance to heal."

"When would you start?"

"As soon as possible, Matron said."

Satchel plumped the last piece of clothing onto the pile and looked at his mother. "It would be good," he said, "if your hands were fixed."

"Yes," said Laura. "They're sore today."

She hoisted the basket to her hip and Satchel could see that she had decided, and that she was happy, and that he should be happy, too. But he winced at the thought of his mother doing the ghastly work required in a nursing home and imagined soaked mattresses, spit, and soggy, mushy food. "Have you told Dad?"

"I'll tell him now. May as well get it over. He'll make his usual noise, but he'll just have to live with it. I can't run my days around his nonsense."

She took the path that had been stamped through the garden and disappeared behind the veranda's fly-screen door. Satchel watched her go, and was struck by her bravery: how small she was, but fierce. He couldn't decide if she had always been that way, a strong, forthright woman, or if she had simply become so, through necessity. Satchel had been fifteen when William closed the service station, and his memories of his mother, before that time, were blurry. He remembered her cooking and cleaning and bandaging his skinned knees, but he couldn't recall things she must have said to him; he couldn't remember the kind of person she had been.

Before Satchel turned fifteen and before the service station was shut down, William had been no more or less religious than most other men his age: the family had a crucifix pinned up in the hallway, but William did not, as far as Satchel knew, say prayers, and he went to church irregularly. When his father started going around insisting that God *would provide*, people took to saying that William O'Rye had found religion, but Satchel did not think so. Satchel thought William had dropped religion completely, and taken up something much darker.

It was hard to decide when it must have started, because he did not suppose William woke up one morning with his entire future crystallized, as if the voice of his God had murmured in his ear that night. It was more likely it had happened slowly, that signs were there early and had been overlooked. But Satchel was forced to date everything from the day William closed the service station because that was the first day they noticed something was going wrong, and by then it was too late to fix it.

William had drawn together the doors of the garage, fastened the lock of the office, and come, as usual, into the house. "Well," he had said, "that's that. No more."

Satchel had glanced up from his homework. "No more what?"

"No more working in the service station."

"Really," Laura said dryly. "What are we going to live on, then?"

William had answered, "God will provide."

They thought he was joking. But the station had stayed unlit and bolted, and William would not get out of bed. They had a spare bedroom and he took up residence in this. Day after day he stayed there, calling for his lunch and dinner, the door of the room propped open so he could see the comings and goings. One day, bolstered by his pillows, he cut up squares of paper and printed on each scrap the words GOD WILL PROVIDE. He tacked this message to furniture and walls throughout the house. He chanted his favorite verses until he'd memorized them in his head and could draw them out like a sword: *Consider the ravens, who neither sow nor reap: God feedeth them. Consider the lilies, who toil not: God clotheth them. Seek not what you shall eat, nor what you shall drink, neither be ye of doubtful mind: the Lord knows you have need of these things. Seek ye the kingdom of God, and all things shall be added unto you. . . .* Laura tried to take him to a doctor, but William refused to go. He was not, as far as he was concerned, ill in any way. The sad truth was, he said, that everyone else was ailing, for they had no faith in God's promise to provide for His people. No one needed to do anything: it was not necessary to earn money, and hence it was not necessary to work. God would ensure there was food on the table, would attend to the bills, and might even fix the leak in the roof. So Laura took herself to the doctor, and came home with hopeless news. William needed treatment, but treatment could not be forced down his throat. He had to recognize he needed help before anything could be done. William said that Laura was the one with a sickness: she suffered from a lack of trust in her God.

"God!" she had wailed. "God is driving us into the poorhouse!"

"God is testing you," William replied serenely. "Have faith, and He will provide. If God so clothe the grass, which is one day in the field and the next day in the oven, how much more will he clothe you?"

Satchel hated to remember this terrible time, the confusion, the whispering. Laura's friends would come over to discuss the situation and Laura would send her son from the room. He was shocked when he realized that these friends were lending his mother money, money they could not afford to lend and she had no means to repay. He had raged, that day, into William's bedroom. "Get out there and open the garage!" he had roared at his father. "Why are you doing this? What's wrong with you? Open the garage!"

Laura had come running into the room, thrown her arms around her son. She had never been a mother who often hugged or kissed her child, and she was not, now, trying to comfort him. She was trying, he thought later, to contain his anger inside him, as if anger, let loose, would pull the whole house down. "Get him out of here!" William was bellowing. "Laura, get him out!"

Satchel yanked his arms free from his mother. "I hate you," he told William, "and I hate your shitty God. He isn't going to give us anything. You're going to let us die."

"Satchel," Laura said desperately, "come away, Satchel, come away." She'd hurried him into the hall-way as if fearing William would strike him, though William had never done so in all Satchel's life. She'd pushed her son into his bedroom, and he'd slumped down on his bed. He had astonished both his mother and himself when he promptly burst into tears. They were tears he could not control, surging down his cheeks and splattering the floor: he felt like he would cry for years. His mother sat beside him and watched him as he sobbed. "Don't worry about it, Satchel," he remembered her whispering. "Don't let yourself worry."

He wanted to tell her to shut up, that he wasn't a

baby and that words like those were not reassuring to him anymore. What he said was, "I want us to leave here—I want to leave him—"

"We can't do that. You can't abandon people. He's not well."

"But what about us? How are we going to live? Where are we going to get money?"

Laura had sighed, smoothing away a rumple in the blankets. "The service station would probably have gone broke anyway. In a few years, the highway would have finished it off."

"Mum!" he gasped. "He's gone mad! Don't you see? It's not just the service station—he won't do anything! How can we survive? How can we pay the bills? What are we going to do?"

"We'll be all right, Satchel," she promised. "Look at the beautiful things around you. Don't think so much about money. It's a poisonous thing to worry about."

Satchel breathed deeply, his tears slowing now. He wiped his face with his sleeve. Laura hesitated, then rested a hand on his shoulder. "He might get better," she told him. "This might not last forever."

And, in a way, William did get better. He left the seclusion of his bedroom and opened the garage, but not to sell petrol. He had sworn off touching money. But he would repair the cars and farm machinery of friends, and the price they paid for this was to hear from him a sermon on the error of their ways. Farming, though a noble occupation, was turning from the face of the God they evidently didn't trust to care for them. And so, while William got a little better, life for Laura and Satchel grew worse. William's catchcry was unstuck from the walls and began to flutter around the streets, and Leroy Piper was suspended from school when he clobbered cold a classmate who muttered, in passing, to Satchel, the words "*God will provide*."

Moke saw her standing at the end of the driveway and barked to alert Satchel. He had wandered from the clothesline to the chicken coop and into the old stables, but he came out and shielded his eyes against the glare of the setting sun. Chelsea was loitering at the side of the road, looking like she would bolt if she saw any hint of movement within the house she was watching intently. She was shy because she drove the school bus, the job that William used to do, but people were disturbed by William's strangeness and frightened by his reputation, and Satchel knew Chelsea's hesitation was anchored in that fear. It bothered Satchel when he saw people react this way to his father, who was never impolite, who had no mean streak in him, who was not a fighter or a drinker. But he understood, too, that there glittered in William's eyes a cheery, jeery sort of madness, that his stiff, shuffling method of walking spoke of a mind that had lost its fluidity. People were wary of William — Satchel, sometimes, was wary of him — because William was crazy, and no one could expect him to be treated the same as everybody else.

Moke's barking made Chelsea snap her head in their direction, and Satchel waved to her. She scurried up the driveway and as she got closer he saw she was carrying a large softbound book, the cover of which bore scribble. "Hi," she said, blinking fast. "I was wondering if I could talk to you?"

"Sure."

"I won't stay long — I just need a minute — I'm not disturbing you, am I? Tell me if I am, and I'll go."

"I'm not doing anything." He would have invited her into the kitchen and offered her a cup of tea, but he knew Laura was talking to William in there and that Chelsea might prefer to stay outside. He stepped backward into the shadows of the stables, and she followed him to the edge of dimness, where she sat on the barrel of chicken feed and Satchel leaned against a wall.

"I've been thinking about that dog you saw," she began. The light flashed off her glasses as she talked,

73

and flicked the walls like lightning. "The stray one at the mountain, I mean."

Satchel nodded, and watched as she swiped through the book's pages until she reached one whose corner she had folded firmly down. She placed her finger on a patch of color among the writing and asked, "Did it look anything like that?"

He came nearer to look at the picture and she wriggled sideways to give him room. She smelled, he noticed, like lavender: his mother had some powder that made her smell the same. The picture was a coat of arms, and on either side of the central shield were two rampant, stylized, bizarre-looking dogs. "They're not the right color," he said immediately. "The dog at the mountain was tan, not gray."

"Maybe that's because the reproduction is bad. Look at their heads. Look at their ears. Look at their tails — smooth, like a cat's. Look at the stripes on their backs."

Satchel frowned at the image. "I suppose," he said. "I suppose you'd say they were close. The stripes are right, at least."

Chelsea sucked in her breath, and Satchel looked at her. His hands were on his knees and his face was level with hers, and he could see shallow pits in her skin, the war wounds of her ongoing battle with acne. "Don't you know what those dogs are?" she asked. "Haven't you ever seen these animals before?"

He shook his head. "What are they?"

"Satchel, they're thylacines. This is the Tasmanian coat of arms. Those animals are Tasmanian tigers."

He stared at her, and she stared back at him. She had dug her teeth into her lip and her eyes were surreally huge behind her glasses. It made him laugh. "Tasmanian tigers are extinct," he said.

"I know," she whispered.

"They're *extinct*. So it could not have been a Tasmanian tiger. And we aren't in Tasmania, either."

"I know," she repeated. "But look at the picture, Satchel. Look at it."

He wanted to laugh again, to giggle with the absurdity of her seriousness, but while she'd endured one scoffing nobly, she seemed prepared to be offended by a second, so he did as she asked, and looked. He took the book from her, and looked harder. He tried to imagine the drawn animals alive, fleshed out and leaping through the undergrowth, and the resemblance was there. It was strange, and left him, for a moment, with nothing sensible to say. He flipped the book to see its cover and found it was one of Miles Piper's school texts. "Is there anything in here about tigers?" he asked.

"No. It's just a history book. But I was thinking that, when I take the bus to town tomorrow, I could go to the library and try to find something. If you want me to, I mean."

Satchel peered at the picture. The similarity was still there. The printed beasts looked partly cat, partly dog. They were more muscular and thickset than the lanky creature he had seen, but their backs were slashed with stripes from their shoulders to their tails, stripes that reminded him of the splits in his mother's palms. He closed the book and put it down quickly, as if it had become suddenly hot to hold. "It wouldn't be true," he said.

"I know. Thylacines have been extinct for years. For years and years and years. And we don't live in Tasmania."

"It was just a dog that looked like those things."

"Yeah, I know. But I can go to the library tomorrow, if you want me to."

He glanced at her, at her small, upturned, pleading face, the stone-colored eyes gazing at him as if he wielded some kind of power. He couldn't remember anyone ever looking at him like that, and it was embarrassing. Her attention was hungry, draining. "I don't mind," he told her brusquely. "Go, if you want to."

She nodded, her head bobbing cheerfully. She climbed from the feed barrel and had taken a few steps down the driveway when she turned to squint at him and said, "I don't think we should tell anyone."

"No," he agreed. He stood and watched her walk away and smiled grimly at the thought of what people would say, should the local pariah and the son of the local madman get together to claim they'd found a long-defunct creature living, of all places, at the foot of the local mountain.

Laura was setting the table and he looked at her as he passed the door of the dining room: she briefly turned her eyes to him and he understood, from this, that William now knew about the nursing home. They had developed over years their repertoire of loaded glances, and now a quick precise flash from Laura's hazel eyes could forewarn Satchel of his father's mood, could alert him to the calamities or pleasures of the finishing day. William was slumped on the couch in the living room, staring at the carpet, and Satchel took the chair alongside him. "Hi," he said.

"Good evening."

"How have you been?"

"Very well, and I thank you for inquiring."

Satchel considered his father: William's face was set wooden, and his eyes seemed dry, their surfaces parched. The TV guide was on the coffee table, and Satchel spun the paper to face him. "Anything good on tonight?" he asked.

"I have not yet perused the selection."

He scanned the paper. "There's not."

"That would not be untypical."

"Why are you talking like that?"

"Like what?"

"You know."

William's gaze scraped his son and fixed itself once more on the carpet. He said, "I detect nothing abnormal in my speech patterns."

"Hmm." Satchel flicked the guide with a finger, sent it skidding over the table's surface. William sat as if his backbone had been extracted, his head thrust forward, his chest bent to a curve, his upturned hands lying limp beside his knees. He made no move when the guide collapsed at his feet. Satchel watched him carefully. He remembered the day Laura told her husband that she had no option but to return to nursing, the cold fact being that somebody had to earn the money to keep them alive. When he'd heard that news, William had not perched on the couch like an injured vulture. He had ranted and raved and stomped through the rooms. He was appalled that the woman he'd married should have so little faith in her Lord. How could God provide for her, he demanded to be told, when she refused to give Him the chance to do so? He had called upon his God to eye off this disbeliever and William's God was the old God, the God of plagues and tempests, of fire and wrath, a sulky tyrannical juvenile of a God, and William called Him down like a necromancer summoning a demon: it was frightening to think of Him being in the room. Laura was a different person in those days, not yet as resilient as she would become, and Satchel could remember the sound of sobs coming through the walls of her bedroom.

Nonetheless, she was determined. After fifteen years of absence from the profession she needed to do much retraining and this she did without complaint. She applied for a position at the hospital in the big town and was given a place on its maternity ward. Despite her retraining she found the work strenuous, the technology dazzling. She told Satchel she could hear babies bawling in her sleep. Her return to work was the droplet that broke floodgates: word of how deep the family's plight had sunk flowed to Laura's burly brothers, who came to town and bailed William up in the living room. What, they wanted to know, did he think he was doing? Was he mad? Was he really such a lazy, selfish, pointless man? William posed like a martyr, taking abuse the way Sebastian took the arrows. *They believed not in God, and trusted not in His salvation. They believed not in His wondrous works. Bless them which persecute you: bless, and curse not.* Laura steered the brothers into the kitchen for another private conversation, closing the door in Satchel's face. Satchel remembered standing in the hall with his fists tightly clenched, hearing the muffled voices and feeling a seething disgust. He hated it that everyone wanted a piece of the saga and shouldered in for their say, but all the hushed or shouted opinions had achieved nothing, and nothing was getting better. He felt, at that moment, no anger toward his father: for the first time he acknowledged that William was not infantile, but ill, floundering helplessly below the surface of reality. Others, though, would persist in seeing him as a curiosity, a specimen to be inspected under the harshest light: they would peck him, if they could, to death. Satchel decided, at that moment, that he would never leave his mother and father. The front his family presented would be united, as strong as it could be.

All this had happened over eight years ago, and his mother could be fearsome now and his father could be feeble, but little else had changed. Satchel leaned into the cushions, his hands behind his head. The ceiling was centered by a plaster rose that had cracked clean through the middle. He pondered the likelihood of one half falling and landing on the coffee table like the segment of a huge, wizened orange. He let his gaze drift around the room, past the smudgy windows and over the floral furniture, and come to rest on William. "The chain saw," he said. "It's fixed, isn't it?"

"I believe I attended to the repairs several days ago."

"And it works?"

"You will find all internal mechanisms in sound operational order."

Satchel chuckled, and William shot a blue glance at him; Satchel suddenly suspected that his father was doing this deliberately now, as an awkward, playful tease. Five minutes ago he had not been teasing, but he had hauled himself out of the murk that could swallow him and hoped to seem, now, as if he'd never been near the edge of that obscurity. And Satchel was grateful, willing to go along with the pretense. He almost told his father about Chelsea Piper and her tiger, for he knew William would find the story intriguing, but he lost the desire as soon as he went to speak. Chelsea had been a source of amusement for a long time — and so had William, and so had Satchel himself.

Laura came to the door, her hands at work behind her back, loosening her apron. "Dinner's ready," she said. William looked at her slyly.

"I hope you didn't set a place for me."

"Well, I did. Aren't you eating tonight?"

"I certainly am. Not here, however. I have a dinner engagement with some friends. Didn't I tell you about that?"

"No, you didn't." She clutched her apron and said to Satchel, "Dinner."

He stood, but William stayed where he was. "Dad—" Satchel started.

"Don't worry about him, Satchel, he's being stupid. Come to the table."

"Your purse," said William. "Is it in the kitchen?"

Laura didn't answer; Satchel trailed her to the dining room, and as they settled at the table, they could hear him in the kitchen, rummaging through his wife's handbag. He would take whatever money he found there and go to one of the town's hotels, where he would drink alone until someone else was drunk enough to join him. Despite his aversion to earning, William had never shown a reluctance in regard to spending. Laura gave him a small weekly allowance, which he usually wasted, buying trinkets that caught his fancy and useless gifts for his wife and son. When he wanted to go drinking or treat himself to a counter meal or add to his collection of expensive paintbrushes, he would dip into Laura's wallet as if this was his personal bank. It was a trait Satchel found deplorable but his mother forgave more readily: it afforded her an evening's rest from him, and gave William something to do.

After dinner, when Laura was watching television with Moke flopped across her feet, he wandered into William's bedroom and looked at the painting his father had been doing that day. William worked at a sloped table that he had designed and Satchel had built, over which a magnifying glass on a mobile arm perched like a robotic mantis. Satchel switched on the lamp and peered through the magnifier. The painting was pinned to the table's surface and had the dimensions William preferred, no bigger than a beer coaster. Joseph had taken Jesus fishing but their poles were lying on the shore, ignored. Instead, young Jesus had one hand dipped in the water and fish were schooled in the hope of being touched. The boy's other hand was held in Joseph's large paw. Joseph, with his free hand, was pointing to the sky. In the sky the clouds had parted momentarily, letting through rays of sunlight that streamed onto the heads of the man and the haloed child. William's work was never subtle, and this was one of his favorite themes: Joseph as guide and teacher, alerting his charge to symbolism that the boy might otherwise fail to see. Satchel's lip curled, and he stepped away.

William had done his best to teach his son that God would provide, and that the trick was to give Him the chance to do so. He had encouraged Satchel to drop out of school lest he be tempted to study for a career. This fired Laura to a degree of fury achieved by none of William's other notions or opinions—when he had declared that he would never die, Satchel remembered, Laura had simply chortled. Now she began to drag her son away when he strayed too close to his father, as if whatever William had was contagious and disfiguring. She was frantic with the idea that Satchel would believe what his father was saying, and it was then that she decided her son should not only finish school, but that he should leave the town when he did so. She said that moving to the city would improve his prospects, but he knew she wanted him gone because with distance, in absence, he would be safe.

He was sixteen then, and looked at his parents as if both of them were mad: one for the temptation, the other for suspecting he could be tempted.

He didn't discuss with anyone the next move he made, not with Laura or with William or even with Leroy. He went to school and cleaned out his locker and walked through the gates for the final time. His father was elated, but his mother seemed to tilt on the brink of hysteria. The next day he took the bus to the big town and got himself apprenticed. William was gravely disappointed, and so was Laura. She had not wanted him to be a tradesman. Like most mothers, she'd hoped for her child the honor and security of a future in medicine, in numbers, in the law. But Satchel had never really cared for school, and his grades had always blended with the average. He wanted an income, and when he got one, he gave much of it to his mother for bills and food and board. His family would be united, but he would share the work of keeping it that way. His mother, he thought, had never forgiven him. Even now, years later, her strongest desire was to make him go away.

He sighed and sat down on his father's bed, hooking

his fingers in its crocheted covering. On the pillow lay William's much-thumbed Bible, its bulk whiskery with slips of paper that marked his favored passages. Satchel picked it up and leafed through it, not bothering to read the comments William had penciled on the soft pages. His father had once collected car manuals, but these ancient words were all the instruction he wanted now. Satchel crinkled his nose, because the pages smelled of must.

He found the quote accidentally, but it jumped out at him like something ablaze. He took a pen and paper and wrote it down and then read it to himself. *But if any provide not for his own, and specially for those of his own house, he hath denied the faith, and is worse than an infidel.* He went to leave the quote somewhere his father would find it, but suddenly lost interest in the idea. William would simply ignore it, and Satchel saved him the effort of throwing it away.

The wagon was cranky in the morning, and the sound of the car's gargling brought out Laura, clad in her dressing gown. Satchel popped the bonnet and together they stared into the blackened mass of the engine. "Spark plugs?" his mother suggested. It was very early, and her breath was foggy with the cold.

Satchel shooed her aside. "I've checked everything. Nothing should be wrong with it."

"It's old. Maybe it's tired."

"If Dad would take a look at it—it wouldn't hurt him—"

"You can take my car."

"I don't want your car. I want this car. This car

would be fine if Dad would just look at it, just for a few minutes, for God's sake . . ."

She would not talk to him in this frustrated, resentful mood, and when he kicked the bumper, she walked back to the house. Satchel threw himself into the front seat and sat for a few seething moments, while Moke stayed wisely quiet and only the chickens clucked on blithely. Satchel closed his eyes and turned the ignition key and the engine caught, as if never having had any intention of doing otherwise.

They took the old road through town and sheared off toward the mountain, the wagon plunging and lurching over shallows in the trail. When they reached the red-gum clearing, Moke pounced away into the scrub and Satchel shed his coat and gathered branches, piling them together near the flat-topped cutting stump. He watched, while he did so, for any sign of the striped animal, and once he spun swiftly when he spied movement in a clutch of fern and strappy trees. But it was only Moke, nose to the ground, running circles around nothing.

The chain saw bucked when he pulled the cord, and the sound was barbarous and everywhere, an ugly gritty muscular howl that careered off the volcano and rattled the leaves in the canopy. A charcoal party of gang-gangs exploded from the trees, clapping the air solidly as they beat for the heights of the mountain.

The racket of the chain saw would be a shock to the things that lived here, like snapping from sleep to find you had woken in a vat of loose gravel.

He sliced the branches quickly and threw the pieces aside. He walked about until he found a log not yet badly rotted, and carved it into portable chunks. He piled up his arms and carried the wood to the wagon, the frost shattering under each footstep. Satchel did not have to think about what he was doing, for he had lived this scene over and over: there was a monotony to his existence that would disconnect his mind as though it were something mechanical. He made many journeys across the clearing and took the same route back again, and by the time everything was done, he was warm and had shaken off his jumper. He flicked his hands clean and pushed back his hair. The sun was high above the land line, the frost had oozed into the earth and the clearing was quiet and empty. He and Moke were alone. "In the car," he called to her. "Come on, girl."

She was reluctant, swerving in any direction but the one that brought her to the car. He smiled as he watched her: she was always busy, a great investigator and explorer. When she was angry, she would raise her hackles and lower her head and look like a wild boar. She skipped through the ferns and over tree trunks, glancing at him sideways, her red tail waving like a torn and ragged fan. Satchel looked around himself, at the boulders cast from

the mountain, at the shadows thrown by the escarp-
ments, at the slick dark soil and the rangy strangled
saplings at the feet of their towering cousins. This was a
place for wild animals, but none of them would show
themselves while he and Moke were here. They would
find him disturbing, but Moke they would fear.

The animal rose and watched the wagon trundle into
the distance, the grass at the roadside whipping its pan-
els as it went. The animal had climbed high into the
mountain in pursuit of a rosella whose flight had been
broken and lopsided, and when the car arrived and the
noise began, it had found itself stranded, unable to
return to the ground unseen. Wary of telltale movement, it had settled into the shade in the hope of
disappearing, and dropped its chin on its paws. Only its
eyes shifted, watching always the progress of the dog in
the scrub. It heard, but did not react to, the sound of
the rosella scraping the mountain's surface, the scrabble
of claws on the rock. Its nose flexed at the scent of
petrol, but this was a familiar thing; the yowl of the
chain saw made it tighten every muscle, but its
instincts kept it lying still. It did not twitch when the
dog turned and looked hard in its direction. Stillness
and invisibility had saved the animal before; if it had
to, it would run for the caves and crevices, and only as a
last resort would it turn to fight. The dog stared for a

prickling moment, its paws planted square on the earth. Then it dipped its head and shook itself, and plowed on through the undergrowth.

Now the disturbance was over and the animal stood and yawned, blinking as the light slanted in its eyes. From here it could see a long way, over the ribbon of highway and into the farmlands beyond. It pivoted its ears, seeking the location of the struggling bird. In several sure leaps, it surged to the flat of the mountain and continued on its way.

The construction of the cultural center took two days longer than Gosling had predicted, and it was the end of the week before the crew packed the equipment to leave. They went to the pub to mark the occasion and invited Satchel along with them. They drank for several hours and some of the men grew nostalgic and maudlin. They spoke of the building as if they had lived and loved within its walls: they forgot how often it had made them curse, how they'd snagged their flesh on its splintery beams, how they'd slipped on the wood in the saturated morning and sweated on the rooftop each day. Satchel sat with Gosling, his chair tipped against the wall. He agreed to play a game of doubles, and he and his partner held the table for three rounds until his partner potted the black. He was glad to return to his seat then, and Gosling bought him another beer. The men pushed coins into the jukebox, punching up songs that were played here over and over again. Songs about wars, about women, about times being hard.

Gosling asked him, "You still considering what I told you? That job up north?"

"Yeah, I'm considering."

"You tell your mother about it?"

Satchel took a lingering sip of his beer. "No, not yet. She's had enough to think about these last few days. She's started a new job."

"Your daddy not making it easy for her?"

"He's being quiet."

Gosling nodded sympathetically. "Sometimes quiet is worse than noise. Well, don't rush it. Tell her when the time is right."

Satchel looked away from the foreman, to the gaudy beating chest of the jukebox. An electrician named Jamie caught up a chair and dumped it and himself in the line of Satchel's vision. Jamie was young, the baby of the crew, gangly and brash and often in trouble: he reminded Satchel of a pup that has not yet learned it shouldn't snap at the sheep, in danger of termination if it didn't learn soon.

"Satchy."

"Hey, Jamie."

"Good times, eh? Good times." The beer sloshed in the electrician's glass, heaving toward the rim. He lit a cigarette as thin as himself and blew out ringed puffy clouds. "Listen, Satchy—your old man's a mechanic, isn't he?"

"He used to be."

"But he fixes stuff? He fixes stuff for people? That's what I heard."

"It depends what's broken," said Satchel. "He doesn't fix everything."

Jamie's head wonked up and down. "Yeh," he said, "yeh. Yeh, I understand that. What—he fixes stuff like generators? He do them?"

"Sometimes," said Satchel.

Gosling had leaned across the table and was listening, a fist wedged under his jaw. Satchel had heard him say that the young electrician had taken volts to the head. Now, "Why don't you tell us what your problem is," he suggested, "and forget all your bullshit?"

Jamie balked, and scratched his scalp nervously, swaying in his chair. He sucked his cigarette. "My dad's got a knackered generator," he said. "Broke down about a week ago. Making it rough for him. We got a guy in to look at it and he says it'll cost two or three hundred to get the thing going. But I heard that Satchel's old man fixes stuff. And that he doesn't like being paid."

"You like being paid for the work you do, James?"

"Yeh."

"You do?"

Jamie's yellow nails fumbled at his face. "Yeh, Gos."

"Then what makes you think Mr. O'Rye doesn't like being paid for the work he does?"

The electrician's lips quivered. "That's just what I heard, Gos."

"You heard wrong, then."

"I mean—what I meant was—he does it out of the goodness of his heart. He does stuff because he likes doing stuff. And he likes just to be paid—a token. You know, you pay him, but not so much he'll be offended. That's what I meant, Gos."

"Jesus, you're a pathetic little weed, aren't you."

Jamie widened his eyes at the foreman and smiled jerkily. Satchel drained his beer and set the glass down. "I'll ask him, Jamie," he said. "Your dad still on that property near the rail crossing?"

"That's the one, Satchy. Gate's opposite the crossing—you can't miss it. Old milk can for a letterbox. Thanks, Satchy. Thanks a lot. I owe you one. You know, the farm's not going good these days; it's a bad time for everyone."

Jamie jumped to his feet and scooped his chair under his arm; his smile faltered when Gosling said, "James. You tell your daddy to pay Mr. O'Rye properly, hear me? I know your dad, and he's not so bad off as some. Mr. O'Rye isn't a charity."

"Right. Right, Gosling—"

"Jamie," said Satchel, and the young man turned to him a face full of stressful panic. "Don't give any money to my father, all right? Don't even mention it to him. He doesn't like talking about it. When you've got the money, you come and find me, and I'll take care of it."

Jamie giggled. "Oh, right, I get you. Give you the money and it's drinks all round. Yeh, I get it, Satchy."

"Just do what you're told, you moron," snapped Gosling. Jamie nodded repeatedly, backing steadily away. Gosling shook his head wearily. "If I was his father," he said, "I'd have drowned him at birth."

"You're a hard man, Gosling."

"I can't abide a fool, that's my problem. And everywhere I look, I see more than enough of them. I don't mean people like your father, Satchel, I mean the genuinely stupid, the ones born that way. Now get me another drink before I remember I'm unemployed. Better get yourself one too."

Satchel pushed himself from his chair and went to the bar. He passed the electrician, who stepped aside for him and said, "Thanks again, Satchy, I owe you. I mean it, you know. We've got to help each other out, don't we? Any time you need a favor, you just ask me. Anything I can do, I'll do."

"Yeah," said Satchel, "I know."

At home that night, when the advertisements came

94

on TV, his mother took her attention from the screen and said, "So the work's finished now, is it?"

"It is for me."

"Does Gosling think there will be anything else? Something for you to do?"

"No," said Satchel. "It's quiet at the moment."

"Oh, well." She was sitting on the couch, her hands spread like bird's wings on her lap. Before her skin had started to crack, she would knit while watching television, turning out cardigans for William and booties for local bazaars: but it hurt her to hold the needles now, and her hands, unoccupied, twisted and fidgeted.

William was sitting at the table, framing his latest painting. He was pretending he couldn't hear their conversation. Satchel had told him about the ailing generator, and he had heard that, had rung Jamie's father immediately, eager to be of assistance. William liked to feel needed. He delivered wood to the elderly and cleaned blocked drains for them; he'd paint their outdoor furniture and dig holes to plant their trees. He had badgered the town council to give him the task of driving the school bus because the responsibility would make him useful: since he did not want the wage that came with it, they gave him the job gladly. When he decided the students would learn more from a day at the mountain than they would cloistered in the classroom, the authorities were not so pleased.

But he didn't like to hear his wife and son discussing work, and never made inquiries about how their day had been. He turned, now, and held up the picture for their inspection. "What do you think of that?" he asked.

"Lovely," said Laura.

William gazed at his handiwork, smiling proudly to himself.

———

Chelsea rang to ask if he would take her to the mountain, and he agreed to pick her up in the morning. The station wagon was difficult to start, and Moke was stubborn about vacating the seat within it, so he was running late and flustered when he finally pulled up alongside her, standing on the corner of her street where she'd wandered while she waited. "I'm sorry," he said. "It's this bloody car—"

She bundled herself into the passenger seat; he noticed, with some trepidation, that she carried a sheaf of papers. "Can't your dad fix it for you?"

"He could, but he won't. He went off cars a year or so ago. He'll still fix machines and engines—tractors, things like that—but not cars anymore."

"Why not?"

"I don't know." He checked his mirror and nudged the wagon onto the road. "I suppose they remind him of what he used to do. Back when he was a sinner. Who knows. No one knows what he thinks."

Chelsea said nothing for the rest of the journey but sat up straight and primly, staring out the window as if what she saw was very interesting. She'd dressed with determination against the blustery cold: she wore a scarf, a jacket, and a pair of woolly gloves, and she had a knitted beanie clamped down on her head. She looked, to Satchel, like a chubby, multicolored, rather grave snowman. She looked like she considered the weather a deadly enemy. She smelled pungently of lavender, and he imagined her dousing herself with powder until her flesh was pure white. He rubbed the windscreen with the cuff of his sleeve, squinting to see through the haze.

They turned off the old road, and the mountain hunched in front of them, its flat peak swathed by fog that was thick and smoky, as if the rock were smoldering. Satchel wondered if anyone other than himself regularly used this uncomfortable, overgrown, almost obliterated track, and what they would think if they saw him and Chelsea Piper traveling along it together. "I came out here yesterday," he told her, more to break the silence than anything, "for wood. I didn't see anything. Moke scares everything away."

"Dogs," she said solemnly, "were used to catch Tasmanian tigers."

"Really?"

"Farmers used dogs to track them, and attack them. Dogs killed lots of thylacines, but I couldn't find a word about a thylacine killing a dog. Tigers lived all over Australia for thousands of years, but it was the dingo that wiped them out on the mainland. Dingoes are just like dogs, pretty much."

Satchel rolled the wagon into the misty clearing and pulled up the brake. Chelsea swiped her glove around the window and gazed through the glass.

"Here? This is where you saw it?"

"Just over there."

"It's the right sort of place," she acknowledged thoughtfully. "Tigers lived where there was scrub, so they could have shelter and hide, but they needed open land too, for hunting. It's quiet here, and safe. It's in the boundaries of the National Park so it's protected, and it's a long way from the picnic ground."

"No dingoes, either."

"No, dingoes have never lived here."

"Probably some feral dogs, though."

She frowned at him, her brows dipping behind her glasses. "I've never seen a feral dog around here. Not even once. If I were a thylacine, this is where I'd want to live."

Satchel opened his door and trudged through the bracken, the air like a razor against his throat. Chelsea followed him, fussing with her papers. "Here," he said, halting. "This was where it was when I saw it. It stepped around this clump of grass and stopped and looked at me."

Chelsea picked her way to the spot and crouched, examining the blades and the wet earth. Satchel looked down at the vibrant colors of her beanie and wondered how long she would force him to stay here, shivering. She tilted her head and stared at him, as if she had heard the thought. She asked, "Don't you think it's amazing, Satchel? If what you saw was a thylacine, you saw something that is meant to be *extinct*."

"I saw something," he answered, "but maybe I imagined it."

Chelsea puckered her face. "You didn't even know what a thylacine looked like, but you saw one anyway. You told me you had seen a dog, and you knew you hadn't imagined it. You believed in what you were seeing, when you thought all you saw was a dog."

He couldn't think of a reply to that. Chelsea straightened, smearing raindrops from her gloves, and headed back for the clearing. "Dingoes never got to Tasmania," she told him over a shoulder; she had to lift her feet high to clear the spikes of the grass, and her smooth-soled riding boots slid on the moss of buried rocks. "The thylacine did, because some of them crossed the land bridge that used to hook Tasmania to the mainland. But the dingo never crossed it because the sea levels rose about thirteen thousand years ago, and the land bridge disappeared into the strait before the dingo reached it. Tasmania became an island then. Thylacines went extinct on the mainland about three thousand years ago, but they survived in Tasmania because there were never any dingoes there to compete."

"You've been doing a lot of work."

"Yes," she said, standing still, "it's given me something to do. Even if it wasn't a tiger, it's given me something to do."

He nodded, understanding, but still he was surprised: she had never seemed to have enough interest in living to ever find herself bored. He knew that boredom was a continual and grinding burden in a small town, and that it pressed most heavily on girls. Young men brightened their days with sport that was played with great drama and seriousness—when Leroy's doctor told Leroy that his football days were over, that his knee could stand no more hideous dives, the town had gone into mourning for the loss of its best rover in decades—and as they got older, they could swap the playing field for the local hotel, where they would find their former teammates reliving shameful robberies and sublime victories. Young women, however, were not encouraged to thus enliven their existences. Many of them left school early, and held part-time jobs at supermarkets and Bargain Bins until they were sacked at eighteen by bosses unwilling to pay them an adult's wage. Many, still children, produced children themselves, and lived tired, rundown lives in rundown, tired houses. Chelsea did not live such a life, but he wondered what she did do, in the long hours between taking the students to their school and bringing them home again. "I wanted to find out what happened to them," she was explaining, and he nodded distractedly. "When something doesn't exist anymore, you can forget it was ever here at all. You forget that it was real. It becomes something make-believe. Like a unicorn. But the tiger wasn't a pretend animal; it was real. I wanted to know why it isn't supposed to be here."

She sat on the edge of the chopping stump, which bore the fresh gouges of the chain saw's whirling teeth, and hung her head. "I'll probably end up making an idiot of myself," she said. "I shouldn't have even bothered. And—I shouldn't have dragged you out here, you're cold—"

"I'm all right," he said. He brushed a rock clean of leaves and spider skins and sat down, clutching his freezing hands together and crimping his toes in his boots. "Keep going."

"Are you sure? Because I'd understand, if you want to leave—"

He shook his head, but she eyed him anxiously. He waited, and she looked again at the earth. "The thylacine must have been happy in Tasmania," she said eventually. "It was the top carnivore. The books say there probably weren't very many of them because Tasmania is small, and a small place can't have many big predators or it runs out of prey. But the tigers lived, and nothing bothered them, and they survived."

She paused to consult the papers she had wedged in her jacket pocket, reacquainting her memory with the facts. It must have taken her hours to fill the lines with her bulging, babyish handwriting and he pictured her at the library, her hair piled around her hands as she wrote, the creases in her forehead denting deeper and deeper. The big town's library was housed in a sprawling, gracious building; when Satchel was a boy, it had regularly sent a busful of books to his town, for the borrowing ease of the locals, and its arrival had been a highlight of the week. The service, however, had been discontinued years ago. "An explorer named Abel Tasman landed on the island in 1642," Chelsea was saying. "No one had discovered the place before him, so he called it Van Diemen's Land. They changed its name later, to Tasmania. When Tasman's sailors went on to the land, they saw paw prints that looked like they'd been made by a tiger, and that's how the animal got its name."

"And because of the stripes?"

"And maybe because it looks a bit like a cat. They gave the thylacine a lot of different names. They called it a hyena, and a marsupial wolf, and a striped wolf, and a zebra opossum. They wanted to make it be like other animals, ones that they recognized. But it wasn't like other animals. It looks like a dog because it evolved the way the dog did, living the same lifestyle and using the same skills, but it wasn't related to dogs, or cats, or anything. It was just what it was, the way it needed to be."

The sun had finished its sluggish haul to clear the horizon and now hung, faint and yellow, exhausted. A wren landed nearby, cocked its charming head at them, and wagged its tail wantonly. Satchel imagined ears everywhere, listening without comment, hundreds of unseen eyes upon them. Chelsea's glasses gave her the soulless eyes of a fish—he wondered if she knew. For all the creatures that lived in the district, there were no fish, not in all the creeks and rivers and dams. There must have been, once, but not anymore. If you wanted fish they had to be bought, dead.

"When the British came to Tasmania, about a hundred and fifty years after Tasman found it, they started clearing forests and raising sheep. They brought dogs and horses and cattle, and they brought disease. Sometimes

104

the settlers saw a tiger and sometimes the dogs would kill one. The Aborigines knew the animal and told the settlers what they knew. So people knew that it existed. The thylacine was shy, but it was never invisible."

The wren had whirled away to hop and hop among the branches, incapable of being still for longer than a heartbeat. Chelsea burrowed her hands into her pockets. What did she *do*, Satchel returned to puzzling. When he was building and felling and whittling away his days, how was Chelsea killing time? When he went to the hotels and talked about football, she was never there. Other girls, but not her. Before he'd given up playing, Satchel had been a fullback, and as such he'd had plenty of time, standing about while the game carried on at the opposite end of the field, to survey the gathered supporters. People came from miles to watch the matches, but he could not remember seeing Chelsea among them. She had rarely been a subject of Leroy's conversation and maybe Leroy, too, had no idea what his sister did with her life. She was a mystery, living outside the closed universe of the small town where privacy was peeled like the skin of an apple. She must never have had a boyfriend because he would certainly have heard: two people together could never keep such a thing unknown.

"Pretty soon, sheep started disappearing or being found dead. The tiger was probably killing some of them, but there were a lot of dogs running free, and rustlers who stole stock at night. But the graziers blamed the tiger. It was a strange animal to them, and because it was strange they didn't trust it or want it around. Someone decided that, one year, thylacines had killed fifty thousand sheep in an area along the coast. So, in 1830, something called the Van Diemen's Land Company decided to pay a bounty on tiger scalps. . . . What's a land company?"

He blinked, bringing himself back. "I don't know. I suppose it owned, or grazed, a lot of land."

Chelsea dipped her head, the sun going white across her glasses. "I didn't bother to find that out," she said apologetically. "I could, if you want me to."

"It doesn't matter."

She pressed her lips together and scrutinized her papers. She was becoming uncomfortable on the chopping stump and shifted, her padding of clothes rising and slumping around her. "This land company already employed thylacine trappers, but now it wanted farmers to hunt them too. It offered five shillings for a male tiger's scalp and seven for a female's. You didn't get more money if you killed any pups she had with her. Five shillings was a lot of money in those days, as much as a workman could earn in a day. And when somebody had killed twenty tigers, the payment went up. Then they gave you six shillings for a male, and eight for a female. And it went higher, one shilling more for every seven extra tigers, until the most a person could get was ten shillings for a male and twelve for a female. I don't understand why they had that complicated system."

"The more tigers died, the scarcer they became," said Satchel. "If a hunter wanted to earn more money, he would have to start hunting as hard as he could."

"So they offered higher prices, to make sure people kept killing?"

He nodded, and Chelsea bit her lip. "God," she breathed. "They really wanted it gone. They wanted to wipe it out. It wasn't even an accident. They did it on purpose. How . . . cruel."

Satchel drew his knees up and linked his hands around his shins. He felt a touch of warmth on the flesh between his shoulder blades where his collar dipped away. The sunlight on Chelsea made her sallow face luminous. Maybe someone had kissed her once, in a dark room's corner somewhere, and he hoped it hadn't been a Judas kiss that had later been used against her, affection as a decoy, a kiss to entrap. Surely she was too wary to let that happen to her, too conscious of her status as a joke. Walled out on every side, she would never find love here.

"Almost sixty years later the farmers were still whingeing about the tigers, and the government decided that it would start paying a bounty too. Lots of the men in government were graziers, you see, so they had an interest in dead thylacines. The government paid bounty for the next twenty-one years. It's hard to say how many tigers died during this time, but it must have been thousands, maybe tens of thousands. Not all of them died for a bounty: they were killed for collectors and museums, and they were caught to make waistcoats from their skins, and a lot were sold to zoos and died. They never bred in captivity. But the government did keep a record of its bounty, from 1888, when eighty-one were paid, to 1912, when three years had passed without paying any. In 1900 it paid over a hundred and fifty. In 1905 it paid over a hundred. In 1908 it paid seventeen. It's thought that a disease, brought in on the boats, might have caused the drop in those three years, because animals hunted to extinction usually disappear gradually, not suddenly. Other species got this disease too, but there were enough of them for some to survive it. They weren't being hunted at the same time, like the thylacine was."

She looked at her notes, but he saw she wasn't really reading them, that she knew these figures off by heart. "In 1909," she said, "the government paid two tiger bounties. The year after that, none. None, and none. There were never any more."

She wrung off her gloves, revealing pallid blotchy hands, and smoothed the papers on her lap. There were orange wafers of fungus growing on a trunk within his reach, and Satchel picked at it, covering his fingers with its dustiness.

"The last tiger to be killed in the wild was shot by some hillbilly in 1930. The last captive tiger died in Tasmania on the seventh of September 1936. It was named Benny, Benjamin. He had been brought to the zoo as a baby with his mother and his brother."

She sniffed, but not because she was crying: the cold had made her nose run, and she blotted it dry with a tissue. He remembered that she had not cried on the occasion when she was most provoked to do so, when she'd worn her dreadful badge to school, and he wondered what would make her give in — a movie perhaps, or sheer frustration. Yes, that was right: he could imagine her weeping as the credits rolled over some tearjerker, luxuriating in the pleasure of it. She could let herself cry for make-believe, but not for anything real. "That's basically the end of the story," she was telling him, "except for one thing. The government realized, at some point, that the tiger had become rare, and they thought it was time to do something about it. On the tenth of July 1936, they declared the thylacine a protected species. Fifty-nine days later, the last known tiger — Benjamin, the one in the zoo — died. He was twelve years old."

She looked at him through her huge, ash-colored

eyes. "The thylacine is officially extinct now. No convincing evidence has ever been found that says any different. But people have been claiming to have seen them for years. Since the last tiger died in the zoo, people have seen them everywhere."

"But no evidence."

She dabbed her nose. "No."

"That's a problem, don't you think? If the animal was living, something would be found to prove it. Someone would hit one on the road or find bones or a fresh carcass. Even a footprint. But there's been nothing."

"Maybe it's careful now," she suggested. "Maybe it hides. People find new animals all the time, animals that have been around for ages but no one's discovered before. These aren't weirdo people who say they've seen a thylacine. A ranger saw one once. He didn't want to talk about it, in case people thought he was crazy."

Satchel smiled skeptically; he got up from the rock and walked around, his legs unbending painfully with the cold. "All right," he said, "let's say they did survive in Tasmania. That's possible, maybe. But I can't believe they still exist on the mainland."

"Lots of the sightings have been on the mainland."

"But you said it yourself: the dingo drove them out about three thousand years ago. That's a long time. A long time, to pretend to be extinct. A long time, to hide every single scrap of proof that you're alive."

Chelsea sat silent, watching him pace through the grass, the tough brown stems of the ferns cracking under his steps. Eventually she said, "What about you? You saw something that looked a lot like a thylacine. Do you think you've gone mad?"

"I might have," he answered. "I've got plenty of reasons."

"Me too," she said, and he looked at her. He knew she felt her alienation, but it was jarring to hear her acknowledge it. She smiled, as if to lessen his awkwardness, and he glimpsed her small, tidy teeth.

"Will you look at these, Satchel?" she asked. "Will you look at them, and see what you think then?"

She proffered some papers, and he shuffled through them, seeing photocopied pictures of thylacines. Rather, it was a single thylacine, the same animal snapped in different positions with the background always the same. It was a caged tiger, and the space behind it was a maze of wire. It did not appear frightened but it seemed aware, and world weary. It had not always chosen to look at the camera and he imagined the thwarted photographer, fruitlessly clicking his fingers. Always, it stood against the wire that hemmed it in.

"The thylacine was about the size of a labrador, but much leaner, more athletic," she said. "It was a marsupial, and it ate birds and other marsupials. It had a pouch that faced backward, possibly to protect the babies from being scratched by the undergrowth. It was a yellowy-tan color, except for the fifteen to twenty dark stripes crossing its back from its shoulders to its tail. It had teeth like a dog, but it had more of them. The tail was long and it didn't wave, like a dog's does— it was more rigid, like the tail of a kangaroo. It sat like a dog and lay down like a dog, but it could also use its tail for support and stand upright, like a kangaroo can, with its forelegs off the ground. It didn't howl or bark, but it growled, and it could make a rough, coughing sort of sound. It could open its jaws wider than any other animal except the snake, over one hundred and twenty degrees. Satchel, look at it."

She finished in a whisper, running out of air. She had stepped off the chopping stump and come close to him, her fingers hovering above the images. She looked into his eyes now, pinkness in her cheeks, pasty and earnest and reeking of lavender. "Was that the animal you saw?"

He straightened the papers and handed them to her. "If you want to believe that it was," he said, "isn't that enough?"

"No, it's not. Satchel, are you afraid I'll think you're stupid? Because I wouldn't. I wouldn't think you're stupid, and I don't."

Her plaintive eyes were searching his face. He

sighed, stalling, shrugging his coat around him. He groaned, "Chelsea, why is this so important to you?"

She blinked, her eyelids like shutters. When she spoke, her words were hushed. "Can't you imagine what it would be like, Satchel, if we discovered this animal had not gone extinct? That something could be found, when everyone thought it was lost? That it's here, when we thought it was gone? It would be a thing of such . . . *hope*. It would mean that the world is a better place — at least, that it's not as bad as it seems. That *we're* not as bad as we seem. It would be like — *forgiveness* — for some of the things that we've done wrong."

He stared at her; she lowered her gaze and muttered, "I can't explain it very well."

Satchel turned to look at the mountain. The sun had burned off the morning's haze and the solidity of the loftiest peaks was clear against the sky. A hawk or a kite was riding the thermals, but nothing else was moving. He wished the animal would walk out from where it was hiding, that he could whistle and it would come. She could see it for herself then. He wondered why she craved forgiveness, what she imagined she had done wrong: she was surely the least sinning of creatures, so meek that her footprints barely preserved in the muck.

"It's cold," he sighed. "We're both cold. Let's go."

He headed for the car, and she hurried after him,

lunging clumsily through the grass. "Thank you for bringing me here," she said. "Thank you for letting me see it."

"I don't own this place. You can come here whenever you like."

He turned the key, and the wagon jumped and started, taken by surprise. Chelsea dropped into the passenger seat, her clothes massing around her. She said, "I know something you don't know."

"Don't tell me," he replied. "I don't want to hear."

He twisted to see behind him and crunched the gears into reverse. The car leaped backward, its engine powering, its rear kicking up and its nose snuffling the ground. Chelsea grabbed for the dashboard, and mud spat across the windows. He glanced at her and smiled and the glaze of panic left her face, and she smiled back at him.

That afternoon he went to the big town to do the family's grocery shopping, a task he hated but did anyway. Laura had written out a list, and this he followed obediently, but he added things that beckoned to him. William had a sweet tooth and Satchel threw into the trolley packets of biscuits and a slab of chocolate. Laura liked things that made Satchel and his father flinch: dates, dried apricots, almonds in their bitter skins. Satchel favored nothing in particular, but he stood a long time before the dazzling selection of dog foods, wondering what Moke would choose.

He traveled home along the highway, touching the horn to cars he recognized, taking the old road turnoff and cruising through his town, raising a hand as he passed neighbors on the street. He coasted by the shops and the houses and finally swung into the driveway of the service station, where he dropped his foot from the accelerator and stared in dumbstruck disbelief. There was a car parked by the petrol pumps, and William was in the office.

He left the shopping in the wagon and walked to the house, refusing to let himself run. He walked deliberately, but thoughts were rushing through his head, tripping over each other, sparkling like fireworks. His skin seemed cold and prickly, but inside he felt the welling of an outrageous joy. William was in the office, where he had not been for eight years. There was a car at the petrol pumps, and William was there. William had opened the station. Satchel yanked back the flyscreen door and called, "Mum, you won't believe it. Dad's outside, he must be—"

He stopped. Leroy Piper was sitting at the kitchen table, grinning sleekly at him. Moke had her head wedged under his arm and, at the sight of Satchel, she thrashed around to free herself. Laura was swilling the teapot and looking at him blankly. "What's he up to now?" she asked.

". . . He's in the office."

"Oh, I know. He needs a part for that generator he's working on. He thought there might be one somewhere in the office. Cup of tea? Did you get the groceries?"

Satchel pulled out a chair and sat opposite Leroy. "Hi," he said.

"Howdy."

"You didn't go away for long."

Leroy snorted. "I'm not staying, either. I just came back to get some clothes. A flying visit, is all."

"Is that your car out the front?"

"Nope, I borrowed it. I'm sharing a house with the guy who owns it."

Satchel nodded. He found it oddly difficult to think of something to say, as if Leroy had been away for years, or they had had some tremendous argument. "Found any work yet?"

"Have. Got the first job I asked for. It's not bad. The pay's all right; the boss is slack."

"Good. That's good."

Laura set mugs of tea in front of them. "Where's the groceries, Satchel? In the station wagon?"

"Leave them," he said. "I'll bring them in later."

She took her cup and went out to sit on the veranda, where the sunlight would be boxed and the

116

flooring would be warm. Satchel and Leroy looked at each other. Satchel could hear the clock ticking on the windowsill. "Have you missed me?" blurted Leroy.

"Yeah, I guess. I've been busy."

"Yeah, me too."

"But are you enjoying yourself? Are you glad you went?"

"Shit, yeah." Leroy's face looped into a grin. "It's great."

"You won't be coming home, then?"

"I'll come back at Christmas, on birthdays, times like that. You playing cricket this summer?"

"Probably."

"Maybe I'll come and watch one day."

Satchel looked down at his dog, and scratched her silky ear. Leroy was wearing a shirt he had never worn before: he took pride in his appearance and liked spending money on himself. Satchel was wearing his old clothes, his flannel shirt not tucked in and his jeans going thin at the knees. He asked, "Do you want something to eat?"

"Nah, your mum gave me a toasted sandwich."

"How long have you been waiting for me?"

"Not that long. It was all right—I was talking to your mum."

"Oh." Satchel smiled weakly; Leroy blew on the surface of his tea.

"She says the work you had is finished now."

"Yeah. But something will turn up."

Moke settled at Satchel's feet, curling circular like a cat. Satchel dangled a hand but she was out of his reach. "Your dad," said Leroy. "How's he?"

"He hasn't changed. I don't think he'll ever change. Not now."

Leroy's mouth sagged, as though the verdict was unexpected. He took a sip from his mug, and his gaze roamed the kitchen. Laura tried to keep the house nice, but Satchel was suddenly conscious that the walls needed painting, that the linoleum was lumpy, that the cupboards were streaked with spills. Leroy would not care about this, but it shamed Satchel anyway.

"And nothing interesting has been happening here?"

". . . No."

"No, it never does. Stupid question, really." Leroy laughed roughly. "This place is the end of the world, you know. It's a dark, nasty, dingy little pit where nothing's allowed to happen."

"That's not true."

"No? What's been happening then? Tell me one thing."

Satchel looked at the table's surface, his fingers flexing around his mug. Leroy smiled darkly. "You see. You're going to die here, Satchel. You'll just disappear into thin air."

Satchel shifted and Moke swiveled her watchful eyes to him. Leroy gulped his tea until it was gone and set the mug down. "Come to the city with me," he said. "I've got a house, and it's got a spare room you can have. I'll help you find work. I was talking to your mother about it and she reckons it's a good idea."

"I can't."

"Bullshit. What's keeping you here? You think your mum wants you to stay? She doesn't. She wants you to go. She thinks you'd be better off in the city."

"I know."

"Well, then?"

Satchel sighed. Leroy was staring at him mercilessly, his blond hair draped like bars over his face. "I will go, one day—"

"Why not today?"

"I just can't, that's why."

Leroy grunted, slumping in his chair: Satchel knew he was disgusted, that he found his friend disgusting. He said, "I'm sorry."

"You are not."

"Maybe, in a few months—"

"In a few months I might have forgotten about you."

Satchel glanced at him, saw Leroy was not joking. He felt heavy and, for the first time in his life, he felt old. He stayed mulishly silent, aware that Leroy was waiting for him to say something, was looking at him steadily, refusing, with equal willfulness, to take the words back. Finally Leroy stood, slipping his coat from his chair.

"Look, Satch," he said, "I've got to hook it. I promised I'd bring the car home before it gets late. My housemate's got a new girlfriend, and he wants to take her out. . . . What are you doing tonight?"

"I don't know. I might go down to the clubrooms, see who's there. Maybe I'll just stay home."

Leroy smiled grudgingly. "That's what I'll be doing, staying home. I don't know anyone besides my housemate, and I don't like going out by myself."

"What about the people you work with?"

"They're all married, got brats. They're no use."

"You'll make friends—"

"I've *got* friends. I've got a friend I used to hang around with all the time. We used to go everywhere, do heaps of stuff. But that friend doesn't care about me anymore. He doesn't know what's good for him."

Satchel followed him through the house and out to the car, where Leroy searched his pockets for the keys. Satchel looked at the office: the chain was linked through its door handles, and William was nowhere, gone as cleanly as if he'd never been there and Satchel had simply imagined what he saw. Leroy slid behind the steering wheel and started the engine. He said, "Think about it, Satchel. I'll ring you in a couple of weeks."

Satchel nodded. He walked onto the road to watch his friend drive away and when he could see nothing that he hadn't seen every day of his life, he turned and went into the house.

His mother was sitting on the veranda, and her eyes had drooped shut: she opened them when he let the screen door slam behind him and smiled a little warily, as if she did not really recognize him. "Why did you say that to Leroy?" he asked curtly. "Why did you say that you want me to leave?"

"I didn't say that." Laura yawned into a hand. "I said that I thought it would be good for you if you went."

"I'm not a kid," he said. "I can do what I want."

"All I said was —"

Satchel jerked away from her. He was furious, and he didn't quite know why. "If I want to stay in town," he snarled, "I should be allowed to stay. I'll move out of this house, if you like, but I'm allowed to live where I want. Is that what you'd like — would you like me to move out? Because I will, if you want."

"Don't be ridiculous." Laura gazed at the cup that was balanced on her knee, her fingers slack around the handle. She had dozed off before finishing her tea, and a film of cloudiness was floating on the liquid's surface. "I don't understand you, Satchel. Most people are desperate to get away."

121

"Most people don't live the way we do, do they?"

She considered him, her face passive. "I've never asked you to feel responsible. I've never wanted you to worry."

"You are not me!" he yelped. "What difference does it make to me, you deciding that I shouldn't worry? You don't live my life!"

"And you are not a child, as you say. Please stop behaving otherwise."

It made him snap his mouth shut, made his cheeks flush hotly. Laura put the cup down and looked across the yard. A chicken was sunbathing among the vegetables, its neck crooked as if broken over extended speckled wings. "You're quite right," she said. "I don't live your life. But I want you to have a life. I want you to see things and do things. I don't want you tied to this place. Tied by your father's illness. Feeling you must stay to help me. You will wake up so angry one day."

"I won't!" he spluttered. "Why do you think you know everything about me?"

"I don't. But it's the way I wake up feeling, some days."

Satchel stepped backward, as if she had slapped him. When he was little, she had struck him as punishment for his crimes and mutinies; he felt young again now, and afraid of what she could do. His fury disintegrated in an instant and he asked, "Is it because of Dad and me?"

His mother shook her head. She'd dyed her hair before starting her new job, and the sunlight skimmed it dully, neither reflected nor absorbed. Her hands, upturned on her thighs, were cracked as badly as ever: a week at the geriatric home had done nothing to help them heal. "Of course not," she replied. "But sometimes I think I have lived a very small life, and that makes me angry. It makes me angry to think of you doing the same."

He sat on the veranda steps, silenced by a dousing sadness for her, and for himself. It was almost unbearable to think of his mother classifying her existence as wasted, and to realize she was not wrong. Life had been stingy to her. He loved her, depended on her, he admired her and learned from her, but this had not been enough to give her value in her own eyes. He had always wanted her to be happy, but he had not understood how important it was that she should appear to be so: she had dropped a mask he desperately needed her to wear, and he wondered if he could ever look at her again without feeling a ripping, tearing sense of sorrow.

And, because of this, there bloomed in him a sense of betrayal: she had let her disguise drop with objectionable willingness, indifferent to the fact that this was a desertion and he would have to go masked, now, alone. To revenge himself he said, "I asked you to take me away years ago, but you didn't."

"Don't be tedious, Satchel. I couldn't leave. You know that."

"Then you should know that I can't, either. You should stop wishing I would."

"I will never stop wishing that," she answered.

Satchel glowered. The dozing chicken had woken and was staring suspiciously at them. After some moments it got to its feet and made its way casually through the garden, picking at vegetables as it went. Laura clucked her tongue at it, and the bird ignored her. Satchel could hear Moke snuffling at the gap below the screen door, heard her small vexated whines: Laura called her, and, emboldened, the dog shoved the door and came out running, claws skittering, ears flat and jaw slung. She dived down the steps and drove the flustered chicken before her, her belly to the earth, her teeth nipping the air. Satchel smiled reluctantly. He remembered the day his mother had arrived home and called him out to the car, where he found the small brown bundle that would become his dog. His father, at first, had frowned on the idea of keeping her, but his mother had stood firm. She wanted Satchel to have the pup, and she would not give William a proper reason why. "It will give him something to think about," was all she chose to say. She may have judged their future darkly and the dog may have been a consolation for him, but it had been a relief to know that their lives were under her control now, that the erratic, chaotic mind of his father would no longer hold any sway.

Satchel sighed. "Do you know what I used to wish?"

Laura lifted her head. "What?"

"I used to wish Dad would die."

His mother said reprovingly, "Satchel."

"I didn't want him to die, I just wished that he would. Quietly, at night, no pain. It would have made things easier."

"But still, you shouldn't think it."

"I don't anymore."

"What stopped you?"

He leaned back on his palms, his face turned to the sun. "I'm not sure. Everything has a right to live, I suppose. Just because something doesn't suit you, that doesn't mean it hasn't got a right to exist."

She said nothing, and he looked over a shoulder at her. "And anyway," he added, "Dad might get better. You've been saying that for years. Something might happen. God might provide."

Laura gasped, and burst into laughter. Satchel smiled, always pleased to make her laugh.

William forgave the misguided opinions of his priest, and the O'Ryes went to church again, occupying their usual pew, four rows from the altar. Satchel would not take off his coat, despite his father's pointed glare: he tucked the folds of material around him and twined his fingers against the cold. He did not unlock them to hold a hymn book or to offer his neighbor a handshake of peace. Outside, it was raining, the wind battering the drops against the stained windows angrily as if some natural force despised what the congregation was doing, shut away and murmuring. It was not a steady, useful, drenching rain: it was a storm that would end as suddenly as it started, leaving in its wake broken branches and puddles on the street. On the journey into the big town his mother had remarked upon the blossoming of the spider orchids that she'd seen on her morning walk; the unfurling of their blood-red petals was a sign that winter was finally giving ground to spring, but the cold and dank were always loath to leave, digging in their heels and lurking until summer came, with its scorching force and temper.

Satchel stood, sat down, knelt, and stood again, a ritual he followed without giving any thought. He thought, instead, of Leroy, who would be in bed and sleeping soundly. He would not repent the agitation he had left in the O'Ryes' kitchen. Leroy's mother was sitting some distance behind Satchel's family, and now and then Satchel heard her attempts to stifle an asthmatic wheeze. Leroy's father never went to church, and neither did his siblings, and nor had Leroy himself. Mrs. Piper didn't like that, but she didn't waste her breath to complain. She had been sick for many years, the onset of her illness having been abrupt and without apparent cause, but malady seemed to stalk the countryside and she was not alone with her stubborn complaint. Others had bad hearts, cloudy eyes, constant influenza.

Gosling wasn't here either: he claimed that the Lord heard his prayers six days of the week and that Sunday was a day of rest for both of them. But the big foreman was planted on the fringe of Satchel's contemplations, puffing with impatience as the days went by and Satchel withheld an answer to his offer. When Satchel thought of Gosling, it was with dread: he worried that the foreman would be on the phone soon, or come pounding on the door. He would take no nonsense from William, careless of the trouble he'd cause.

Satchel slid his eyes sideways to take in his mother and father. William had repaired the generator, reinforcing his knowledge that the world could not turn without him, and was sitting straight as a flagpole, voicing the responses with gusto. The elderly woman to the left of him was also sitting rigid, as subdued as William was loud.

Laura, placed as always between her husband and her son, was the only one of the three who used her time in church constructively. Satchel daydreamed and William sought offense, but Laura prayed. He knew who she prayed to: a kindly, lenient, understanding Lord, a youthful Lord, with adaptable ways. He supposed he knew what she prayed about, too, for Laura's life, as she said, was a small thing, and one that lay exposed.

The priest must have been feeling the chill: he had rushed through his sermon and spit-fired out the hosts. He sat in his chair to calm himself, his robes hitched to display a shiny new pair of shoes. Satchel looked to see what his father was making of this, but William's blue eyes were squeezed fervently shut. Satchel turned, instead, to the crucifix suspended above the altar. As a child, the blood and anguish depicted there had thrilled him to the bone.

He thought of the striped animal, and hoped it knew of somewhere that was shielded from the storm. He pondered whether rain was good for it, or bad—if creatures would come out to browse the freshened landscape and make for easy hunting, or if they would shy from the water and the bogginess of the ground and make the animal's life difficult.

Laura shifted, distracting him. She'd finished with her prayers for the day. The priest stood to close the mass, and in those final moments, Satchel shut his eyes and bowed his head. He sent up only a single request, on the wings of his mother's many: God, he prayed, *make it true*.

He could not bear to be unoccupied, and because the afternoon was clear, he dragged the table from the kitchen, disregarding Laura's protests that he was leaving her without a decent working surface. William helped him carry it to the garage, and Satchel opened the big wooden doors, Moke dashing through them to investigate. Dust swirled as the sunlight sloped in, whitening a square of the discolored floor. They shuffled the table to the center of the brightness, and William rested his elbows on its top, exhausted. He had once been a fit man, and strong, but his years of inactivity had softened him and Satchel found the sound of his breathing embarrassing. He looked at his father critically and realized for the first time that, were they to fight each other, William would not win. He wondered for how long this had been the case.

"Anything else?" asked William, and Satchel shook his head. Moke had found something in a corner, but William did not go to see what it was. He turned on his heels and trudged out, bent as a mourner. When Satchel could no longer hear his footsteps, he went to Moke and crouched beside her. She had found the shed skin of a snake, fragile as heirloom lace.

Somewhere in the garage would be things he could use, and he spent an hour finding them, wiping aside cobwebs and dusting with his sleeves. He gathered a sanding block and sandpaper, leftovers from when the house had been painted, and a bottle of timber stain with a cap stuck fast, which had to be soaked before it would twist. He found a brush, its bristles stiff as spines, and ground it between his fingers until it was flexible again. From the back of the station wagon he took his box of tools and rummaged through the metal for his hammer, a chisel, and a screwdriver. He'd bought his tools as individuals, one by one when he'd saved enough to buy the best he was ever going to afford. He went to the big town to get tins of lacquer and paint remover and then, collection completed, he rolled up his cuffs and began.

It took the rest of the day to strip the table of the red paint William had slathered over it, a thick oily paint that had seemed, at some time, too good to go to waste. It had scarcely chipped in its years of service, but it buckled under the paint remover, wrinkling and writhing. Satchel scraped it off and smeared it onto newspaper and scrubbed the remaining traces with sandpaper. The table stood as if naked then, as vulnerable and pale as skin exposed to sunshine for the first time in months. He had already switched on the garage light, but it was becoming too dark to see clearly so he whistled to his dog and shut the doors for the night. Laura was still grumbling, so he brought the card table in from the laundry and unfolded it in the kitchen for her.

The next day, after waving his mother off to work, he opened the doors again and took up the screwdriver. The screws that joined the legs to the surface were long and their threads were wearing; he cleaned those that could be salvaged and replaced those that could not, and he slotted each into its tunnel and tightened them until the timber creaked. The table's top would dip irritatingly if weight was placed on a particular corner, and this fault he fixed with a chock of wood that he glued and then screwed into place. The new stability was satisfying, and he wished he had attended to the problem years ago.

Then, he sanded everything icy smooth. Particles fell in clouds, catching in Moke's feathery hair and wafting into ripples over the concrete floor. Satchel stopped thinking, his eyes on the hand that held the sanding block and sent it back and forth along the grain, his mind lulled by the repetitiveness of the work. When Moke barked, he jumped as if stung.

"Hi," peeped Chelsea.

It was almost a week since he'd last seen her: her unannounced and unpredictable appearances in his life were disruptive and bizarre. She was like a goblin who stepped from behind a leaf or a ghost that materialized from thin air, whispered madness in his ear and vanished once again. He said, "You gave me a fright."

It seemed a childish thing to say, and he would have liked to take it back. She looked sheepish and shuffled sideways. He expected to hear her usual offer to leave and come back another day, but she said nothing, so he took up the block and slid it down the rail of the table. "I found out what you knew and I didn't," he said.

"Were you glad to see him?"

"Sure."

"I wasn't. He thinks he knows everything now he's living in the city."

Satchel smiled. He blew on the table and roused a fog of particles. "What have you got to tell me today?"

"You're never going to believe it."

He straightened and looked at her. Her hands were clasped and tucked under her chin, and her face was lit with excitement. "Well," he said, "come in."

He wiped the table, and she perched on one corner, he on the opposite. She did not smell of lavender today, but of horse and hay, which was easier to breathe. While she talked, he toyed with the dusting cloth, unraveling its woven hem. Moke lay under the table and watched each loosened thread drifting to the floor.

"Remember," she said, "how I told you that people are always claiming to have seen the thylacine, in Tasmania, and here, on the mainland?"

"But no proof has been found."

"Right, nothing. In 1937, a year after the last captive tiger died, people started looking for them. A search party was organized in Tasmania. They found paw prints in an area where thylacines were known to have lived, and they asked that the place be made into a sanctuary, but it wasn't. They asked twice, and both times they were refused. A few years after that, another search found nothing. If tigers had been living in that place, they weren't there anymore. They weren't anywhere. They were gone. People kept searching for them, though, and they still do. In Tasmania they put out baited cages, and hook up cameras along animal trails, and make sandpits for footprints. Some of these searches last months, even years. One search set more than four thousand snares in a few months."

"What did they catch?"

Chelsea paused. "Well, no thylacines. But since 1936, there's been thousands of sightings. Not just one or two — thousands. Even now, there's usually three or four a year. Some of them have been wrong — they say the animal has a bushy tail, or long ears — but some have been right. I mean, some have mentioned things about the tiger that aren't so well known, things like the huge jaws, or the way it can stand like a kangaroo."

"You found out about those things. Anyone else could too."

"Yeah, they could, but why would they bother? Why make up a story about seeing an extinct creature when you can't prove anything and most people would laugh at you?"

Satchel grimaced, and resumed shredding the cloth. Chelsea brought her feet up and sat cross-legged on the table. She was wearing leather sandals and her clubby toes were exposed and white with the cold: she had painted their nails a ghastly shade of green. "On the mainland," she continued, "everything says that the tigers died out about three thousand years ago. All the remains that have been found, the bones, the mummified carcass, the cave paintings — they're all at least four thousand years old. But sightings of tigers are always coming in, from every single part of the country."

"But no proof. Thousands of years, but not one bit of proof."

"Some people say it's a conspiracy. That proof is found all the time but it gets covered up."

Satchel laughed, and Chelsea allowed herself a tolerant smile. When she thought he'd had amusement enough, she leaned closer and said, "But listen, Satchel. Remember how, the other day, you said you might believe the tiger survived in Tasmania, but that you couldn't believe it survived on the mainland because it has been gone from here so long? Do you still say that?"

"I guess."

Chelsea looked cagey. She glanced around the garage as if spies slunk in every corner. "Listen to this, then. Around the turn of the century, when the boun-ties were killing thylacines, there was also a trade in live tigers. They were trapped and sent all over the world, mainly to collectors and zoos. Do you think some of them were sent here, to the mainland?"

"I don't know. Maybe."

"Probably. They probably were. There's a record of sixteen thylacines that were supposed to come here, and they probably did. And these tigers were meant to be released into the bush, to start a wild population. Records weren't kept well and it's impossible to say what happened exactly, but maybe what was meant to happen did happen, as it should have. Maybe they were set free, here."

Satchel looked away from her, gazing down the driveway. Chelsea let a minute go by before she spoke again.

"If you admit tigers might have survived in Tasmania because it's not such a long time since they were living there," she said, "you've got to admit they could have survived on the mainland too, if they were brought here just as recently."

"Dingoes drove them out of here the first time," he reminded her. "How would tigers live with dingoes?"

"They wouldn't have to—not if they were released where there weren't any dingoes, where there had never been any dingoes. A place a lot like this place, in fact. The sixteen thylacines were supposed to be released in an area about four hours by car from here. You could go there right now, and be home again before bedtime."

He stared at her, his fingers tight around what was left of the cloth. Chelsea's teeth were pressed into her lip, and her eyes were as large as plates.

"They could have come here," she whispered. "They could travel the distance, over that many years. If those records are right, and those thylacines really were set free on the mainland, they could have walked here and found the mountain and decided to stay. The tiger you saw could have been a great-great-grandchild, or something like that. And where there's one, there must be others."

They heard the sound of footsteps and she sprang to the floor, blundering against the table. William appeared between the garage doors and grinned at the pair of them. "Hello," he said. "I thought I could hear voices."

"Hello, Mr. O'Rye," croaked Chelsea.

He made no move to enter the garage, hovering by the doors with his hands on his hips. He had slicked his dark hair down severely, and greased it with something that mapped the path of the comb. And he was squinting, unable, against the dimness of the building and of his eyes, to see them distinctly. Satchel was sometimes bothered by the thought that there was something indefinably ludicrous about his father's appearance, and he thought it now. "How do you like what Satchel's doing to the kitchen table?" William asked Chelsea.

She seemed confused, and cast Satchel and the table a fleeting, panicked glance. "It's a nice table."

"Hopefully it will be nicer soon. But I think it's a shame, really. When you take the paint off something, you're taking away some of its history. We've eaten a lot of breakfasts on that table, but it's not the same table now."

"It's a better table," said Satchel. "It doesn't wobble anymore."

"But that was part of its character, I thought. It had personality. We all need a few wobbles. Wobbles are the spice of life."

Satchel looked dour and said nothing; Chelsea gave a stumbling laugh. William smiled generously, as if he'd given amusement to her like a gift. He asked, "What were you two talking about, anyway?"

"Leroy."

William slouched from one foot to the other. "Leroy. A boy with many a wobble indeed. Cup of tea? Coffee?"

"No."

"Pardon me but I wasn't asking you, Satchel. I was asking your guest."

"No thanks, Mr. O'Rye," said Chelsea.

William nodded deeply. "All right. Sing out if you change your mind. Goodbye, then."

He took a step away, and a step back again. "You wouldn't care if I stayed and talked with you, would you? I'm a bit bored."

"We would," said Satchel. "Go away, Dad."

"What about if I just sit here and listen?"

"Dad!"

He went, sag-shouldered, and they sat silently while his footsteps ebbed away. Chelsea licked her lips nervously. "I thought—I thought he might say something about the bus."

"He wouldn't."

"But he probably doesn't like me —"

"Forget about him," Satchel said sharply. His father's interruption had frizzled the mood and he stepped from the table, snatched up the sanding block. Chelsea watched him inspect the wood and use a fingernail to remove a sliver of paint caught in a shallow. She said, "I think it looks nice, this table. I think you've done a good job."

Satchel muttered, "Thank you."

Chelsea scanned the garage. The shelves on the walls were set in shadows, the windows insufficient for the size of the building. It was strewn with the clutter typical of its purpose and the air smelled of oil. Beyond the table a great hoist was bolted to the floor, lowered as far as it would go. Moke, flat out beneath the table, swished her tail politely when Chelsea looked at her.

"Satchel," she said eventually, "I believe you. I think you saw something amazing."

"You're the only one who would."

"Not if we can prove it."

He had crouched to inspect the underside of the table, and he ducked his head to see her.

"If we could catch it," she said, "everyone would believe you."

He wiped his fringe from his eyes and watched her wander around. She said, "Imagine what it would do for this town, if we could prove that thylacines are living here. This place would be special: everyone would want to come here. People would travel from all over the world. The highway would have signs along it, pointing out the way. This town is going to collapse one day—it's already dying. But thylacines would save it. They'd stop it from disappearing, that's for sure. And we wouldn't disappear with it."

She butted a heel against the hoist, and the steel gonged dully. Satchel's hands were gray with grit from the sandpaper, and he dragged them across his knees.

"I think it should stay here," she continued absently, "not be sent to a zoo or something. We'd build a big cage for it, make it all nice and natural, put it where it can see the mountain. We'll sell photographs of it, and have a tourist place where people can buy things and learn about the tiger. We'd be famous. Everyone who came here would want to talk to us. Magazines would pay for our story. I'd tell them that you discovered it, but I could say I helped you later, couldn't I? Because I believed you. We might even be on television. We probably would be, I reckon."

She turned to him, her expression suddenly serious. "We'd be rich and famous, Satchel. We'd never have to worry about a thing, not for the rest of our lives."

Satchel stared at her. He didn't, he realized, know her at all, and he felt foolish for imagining her to be something that she was not. She was no resigned, defeated creature with an embedded desire to disappear. Rather, she still clung fiercely to her old yearning to be recognized, to have her existence acknowledged. She wanted everyone to know her, and maybe she imagined this would make them like her, too. He supposed he should pity her anyway, but he didn't anymore. He turned back to the sanding. "It's hard enough to find the thing," he said, "let alone catch it as well."

"Yeah, but it could be done. You could build some sort of trap. I'd help you set it, and I'd inspect it every morning before I took the bus out, if you couldn't be bothered doing that."

He forced the block against the table, particles of wood dust cascading into his eyes. He said, "I thought you wanted to find a tiger because finding one would make the world a better place. Not because it would make you rich."

She wheeled, and the answer she gave jumped from her defensively, as if he had seen her doing something sneaky and depraved. "I'm just saying that's what *would* happen, *if* we caught it," she said. "If we did, that's all."

"Well," he said, "we won't. That was just a dog I saw."

He thought she might try to talk herself out of her disgrace, but she did not: she remained only a few minutes before deciding she should go home to prepare for the afternoon bus run, and hurrying off down the drive.

*   *   *

For the next two days he worked on the table. He thinned the crimson stain and wiped it into the wood, sponging the excess as he went. When the stain was dry, he popped the lid of the lacquer and painted the table carefully; the following morning he sanded flat the air bubbles and gave it a second coat. When it was complete and dry, his mother helped him cart it back to the kitchen, where its deep glossy surface reflected the light bulb that hung from the ceiling. William came to look at it, bending at the waist so his nose came close to the table. He said nothing, and Satchel watched him watching his own image, the blotted flattened echo of himself wavering in the shine.

After dinner Satchel did the washing-up and his mother did the drying. William went to his bedroom to work on his latest miniature. Laura held tea towels in both her hands, trying to protect her skin. At the geriatric home she had to grind pills into powder before they could be forced down flaccid, tired throats, and her hands were not improving. Now and then he heard her catch her breath as the suds burst against the splits in her skin. "Leave the dishes," he said eventually. "They'll dry by themselves."

When he finished at the sink, he wiped the kitchen benches and went outside. The sky was black but the moon was almost full, and everything was vaguely silver.

142

Moke was sitting on the veranda, and she got up to follow him through the yard, halting at the door of the chicken coop when he stopped to check the birds were safely in their shelter and a stray had not been left outside. One side of the coop was starting to list, and he reminded himself to attend to it before it collapsed completely. He walked down the driveway and collected his tools from the garage before hauling shut the doors. He gave a cursory glance to the remains of the service station, then trudged up the drive again, lifting the hatch of the station wagon when he reached it, and dropping the tools into their box. It was cold outside, and so quiet he could hear the tap of Moke's nails on the cement, but he did not hurry to go inside, where a fire was lit in the lounge room and a movie was beginning on TV. He stopped, and listened to what he could hear. A truck changed gear on the highway, a distant renewal of strength. When he could no longer hear the sound of its engine, he listened harder, but Moke was standing still beside him and the night was absolutely silent. He patted his thigh, and the dog trotted after him into the house, where he locked the door behind him and put the key on the nail.

———————

The animal returned to its rocky bedding at dawn. It loped a zagging course through the grasses, the tip of its tail raised just above the dirt, and when it came to open spaces, it broke into a canter. It was seen, as it went, by many eyes beyond its reach, by magpies who bowed their noble heads and by thornbills who were not distracted from their ceaseless scouring. The animal slowed as it approached the mountain, and raised its head to listen. It sniffed all around the entrance of its home, detecting the scent of those who had passed in the night. A rattle in the trees made it swing its body and stare, its feet stamping nervously, but it saw only a branch rebounding with the departure of some hefty bird. After some moments it turned to the shelter and stepped inside, the hair on its spine ruffling against the roof. The earth was damp at the mouth of the cave and stuck in clumps to its paws, but beyond this the cave straitened into a cramped, dry, cozy space, and here the animal lay down. It licked at a patch of its foreleg, its head nodding rhythmically, until the hair was dark and its eyes were closed. It flopped, then, onto its side, its legs stretching stiffly before curling up to its chest, and fell soundly asleep.

Satchel woke at dawn, his face against the mattress. He groped for his pillow blindly, and his arm slipped from the side of the bed, his knuckles knocking the boards. The slight pain woke him thoroughly, and he lifted his head. He lay precariously on the brink of the mattress and his pillow was doubled over on the floor. His blankets were snarled at his waist, and his shoulders were cold. He did not usually sleep restlessly, and he wondered what had bothered him, what he must have dreamed.

He got up and went to the kitchen, filling the kettle high. Moke stood up in her basket, shook herself heartily and bounced across the room to greet him. Satchel lit the fire, bundling newspaper into spheres and arranging twigs upon them. He flicked insects from the larger chunks before setting the pieces among the flames.

He washed his face in the bathroom while the tea brewed in its pot, the tap water frigid and smarting. The mirror showed his hair everywhere, in urgent need of cutting. He studied his image gravely, his frown denting a crease in the bridge of his nose. His hair was black, his eyes were purple-blue, his face was broad at the cheeks but less so at his chin. He pondered the likelihood that he was ugly, or if some mornings he simply felt that way.

In the kitchen he poured a mug of tea and filled a saucerful for Moke, adding more milk for her than he did for himself. She lapped at the plate untidily, splattering droplets in an arc over the floor. Satchel took his tea to his room and dressed in a hurry, in clothes he'd worn the previous day. He heard his mother cough in her bedroom and tried to move more quietly.

The kitchen was warmer when he returned there; Moke had finished her tea and looked at him expectantly. He unlocked the door, and they both went outside, Moke racing for the privacy of the orchard. Satchel headed to the chicken coop, and the birds were there, grouped together by the fencing and pecking pointlessly at the ground. He wished them good morning, and for the first time in months the words, meeting the air, were not overcast by haze. Spring had made inroads, and the difference between his body's inside and outside was no longer so stark. He threw the grain over the top of the coop, and the chickens went haywire.

He went to the station wagon, and Moke came running, wary of being left behind. He pulled out the choke and pumped the accelerator before turning the key, but the car stuttered grumpily and fell silent.

Satchel sighed, weary of this daily ritual. He tried the key again, and Moke licked his cheek consolingly when he swore. On the fourth attempt the engine fired and he forced his foot against the pedal to keep it that way, careless of the roar that erupted from the car and of the cloud of smoke that exploded from its rear. He imagined his mother cramming her pillow about her ears and the grizzling of William, claiming for himself the right to complain. Satchel gave the engine time to warm and then looked at Moke. "Out," he said.

The dog stared at him unblinkingly, cocking her head in an effort not to understand. Her tail, however, stopped wagging. "Out," Satchel repeated. "Go on, girl."

She went, jumping heavily to the ground. She didn't lose hope as he leaned across to shut the door, ready to leap should he suddenly change his mind. Only when the car was coasting along the driveway did she allow her ears to drop and he glanced in the rearview mirror to see her standing where he'd left her, staring forlornly after the car. It was always a tragedy, in her little life, to be left behind.

He took the old road into town, passing his neighbors' houses and then the darkened stores, past the war memorial with its three deeply inscribed names, the granite oily with the night's drizzle. Satchel loved the morning, the sense it gave him of being alone on the earth. He thought of the striped animal: if it was nocturnal, it was probably sleeping, having scuttled like a vampire away from the sun. Today, at the clearing, he was going to look for it. He had no idea what he would do if he found it. He would not catch it or harm it, but he wanted its likeness locked more securely in his mind.

He was well beyond the flour mill and was almost at the turnoff when some intuition made him dart his eyes to the mirror to see Moke hurtling along the road behind him. He cursed and wound down his window; the car slowed fractionally and the dog increased her speed. Her long hair was streaming, her tongue was dashing at her throat, and her golden eyes were joyful. She could run for miles, he knew. She was a working dog, and stamina was bred in her bones. She could follow him to the clearing at a gallop without the slightest difficulty. He shouted at her as the car flashed past the turnoff. His concentration skittled, he yelled furiously at her, hitting his foot to the accelerator. Moke, encouraged by his voice, flew faster. Her eyes were on him, not looking where she was going. She was directly below his window, and he could have reached down to touch her when she stumbled and went under the car.

He smacked the brake so fiercely that the wagon skidded sideways, its rear wheels sliding on the bitumen and billowing a cloud of dust. He pulled to the edge of the road and ran back to where his dog lay sprawled. She gathered her feet as he got to her and stood herself up, her tail waving slowly. He dropped to his knees and touched her cautiously. Her right hind leg was broken, hinged lop-sided from her hip. He murmured to her as he probed her body for more damage, but she seemed to be all right, and he sat on the road and stroked her forgiving face. She had a white blaze down her nose, and she had lost skin from it, the blood blotting the hair pink. "Dumb dog," he said. His hands were shaking. "Dumb dog," he said, "I'm sorry."

She licked her lips, and her tongue was red. Drops of redness landed on the road and glistened. He looked at her, his flesh tingling, and she retched suddenly, cough-ing out a pool of blood.

He caught his breath and lurched to his feet. Moke limped forward, pathetically determined not to be left behind again. He picked her up carefully, her jagging leg held away from his body. Long red threads were dribbling from her jaw and sticking to her like cobwebs. He carried her to the car and draped her along the back seat, where she stayed for only a moment before shuf-fling to sit upright. He grabbed a sack from the floor and tucked it around her before throwing himself into the driver's seat and turning the key. The engine grunted. He bit his lip and jerked the key and the engine clicked and went quiet. "Start," he hissed. "Damn you, you bas-tard, start — *start* —"

Five times he turned the key, slamming his foot to the pedal hysterically, and on the fifth attempt, the wagon made no response at all. It made none of its taunting noises, and the only sound was Moke's panting and the jangle of the keys as they knocked against each other. Satchel stepped from the car and gazed around. He told himself to keep calm. In the distance he could make out the roofs of shops and houses, smaller than lids of pillboxes. In all the other directions there was nothing but hills and grass, fences and farms and, in one, the black form of the volcano. Nothing was moving except the peaks of the evergreens, which shivered against the wind. He looked at Moke, who had hunched to the seat and dropped her ears when she met his glance. She was drooling blood all over the vinyl. He took her paw and felt it was cold. "Moke," he said, "I'm going to get Mum's car. You have to stay here, but I'll come back for you." He stroked her head and drew the sack closer to her, and shut the car door. He paused just a moment to look at her through the window. She was a pretty dog, and the grubby sacking did not suit her. Her golden eyes were blinking and the hair beneath them was streaked with tears. "I'll come back," he promised again.

And then he heard a sound he recognized, but couldn't say from where. He swung toward the town and saw the school bus burling along the road. It plowed toward him, rumbling contentedly, its broad forehead shimmering in the morning light. He stood on the bitumen and held up his arms, and Chelsea dropped through the gears and brought the bus to a stop in front of him. She pulled the lever that opened the doors and said, "Satchel?"

"Chelsea, you've got to take me to see Joshua, it's Moke—"

She unbuckled her belt and came down the steps. "What?" she asked. He felt a strong desire to shake her, distraught at her inability to understand everything immediately. He clenched his hands and spoke deliberately.

"It's Moke," he said. "I've hit Moke with the car. She's bleeding, and I have to take her to the vet. I have to get her to town, and the station wagon won't start. So I need you to drive me there."

"I can't—I have to pick the kids up for school. They'll be waiting for me."

"No, forget them—"

"Satchel, I'll lose my job. I need this job—"

He clutched his fingers in his hair. "Chelsea," he begged, "please. She'll die. She's going to die. Please."

Chelsea hesitated. She was remembering that they had parted on bad terms: she had gone home and cried because she always ruined everything; everything she touched she spoiled; everything she attempted she failed. She had vowed to return to the safety of her old, mousy, wordless ways, minding her own business, telling no one of her own. That was the life she was supposed to live. She went to the wagon and peered through the window. "I'll take you home so you can get your mother's car," she said, and then, "Oh."

Moke was slapping her tongue around a mouthful of blood. Satchel yanked open the door and dabbed the sack to her jaws. "Chelsea," he said, and his voice was riddled with panic, "please!"

She stepped backward. She was going to say something, but for a second or two she was silent, as if she first had to find words that were hidden, or lost. "I won't," she said faintly. "I won't drive you to town. . . . You will have to get there by yourself."

He looked at her, and she gazed fixedly at him. "Go ahead," she prompted. "Go."

". . . Where are the keys?"

"In the ignition, I suppose."

He gathered up his dog and carried her to the bus, Chelsea trailing after him. He settled Moke on the floor and dropped into the driver's seat. He smiled at Chelsea, who stood in the doorway with her hands in her jacket. "Thanks," he said.

"Don't thank me," she answered. "I'm protesting about this. You're stealing my bus. I hope she'll be all right, Satchel."

"Step away from the door," he said, and she did.

He turned the key and the bus chundered into action; Chelsea moved clear as it pulled away and watched it barrel down the road, swinging toward the highway and quickly vanishing from view. He was driving fast; the bus didn't like being driven fast and it could hold a grudge for days, but she smiled to watch it go. She turned on her heels and began the walk into town. In an hour or a little more, when the headmaster arrived at the school, she would ring him and describe what had happened. He would be annoyed but she would say that none of it was her fault; she had done all she could. Satchel O'Rye was much bigger than she was; she could not physically restrain him. She would tell the principal she had no idea where he might find the school bus but that she expected Satchel would return it eventually. And she would leave it to him to inform parents on distant farmlands as to why, exactly, their children had not yet been removed to school.

In the meantime, while she waited for the time to come to make the call, she would sit on the heater and have a cup of coffee and perhaps eat some more breakfast. She felt intensely happy, and it made her want to run: she couldn't run fast and she moved without grace or style, but she ran anyway.

The animal woke, its ears swiveling to collect sound, their tips bent against the roof of the hollow. It lay in a nest of moss and tangled eucalypt bark, and the trunk of a sugar gum obscured its view outside. It felt but ignored the movement of the creature that was blundering in the darkness behind it, searching for a gap that would allow it to wriggle past the animal's body. The animal sniffed the air thoroughly, opening its mouth so the taste of it flooded its throat. A sparrow perched against the trunk of the tree and fluttered its wings frantically; it fell, rather than flew, from its place, scooping the air before it touched the ground. The light of the sun came filtered through the canopy, but the animal narrowed its eyes against the whitening sky. The hollow was not a desirable home: water could work its way through the ceiling, and the outlook was scrambled with bracken and scrub. An intruder into this territory had cover to conceal its approach until it stood at the door of the den. And the den itself was flimsy, inclined to rattle with the wind. The walls creaked and moaned unhappily. That night, the animal would go in search of a more secure home.

It bowed its head to regard the little creature and, after a second of indecision, clasped its teeth around the slender neck.

Joshua's truck was parked in his driveway, and Satchel pulled the bus in behind it. The vet lived on a small property on the limits of the big town, and he spent most of his days driving around the district, paying house calls and attending those animals that could not be transported to his surgery: mares heaving with difficult births, bloated sheep with stomachs like drums. He was a tall, elderly, pitifully bony man, and he was coming down the steps of his house with his instrument bag thrown over a shoulder when Satchel jumped down from the bus. "Satchel?" he shouted. "What on earth?"

They took Moke into the kitchen, where Joshua cleared the table of jam jars and a box of cereal and Satchel put his dog down gently, sliding his hands from beneath her weight. Joshua hooked on spectacles and bent to examine her. He probed her body with his fingertips and said nothing for several minutes. He filled a syringe with painkiller and slipped the needle in the scruff of her neck. Satchel stood against the wall, nicking a thumbnail nervously. Moke kept her eyes on him, and whenever Satchel moved, she would slap her tail lightly, absurdly devoted. Joshua lived alone, and had a taste for costly objects: on a shelf there was a chunky handsome antique clock, and Satchel could hear the whirring of its innards as it grated down the moments. He could smell coffee beans and insect spray and socks steaming before a fire somewhere, all the odors of bachelorhood. After a time he had to say something and what came out was idiotic. "Her leg is broken, I think."

Joshua scoffed. "Her leg is shattered, young man. And that's the least of her problems. You shouldn't drive so wildly."

Satchel cowered, his arm flopping to his side. He had known Joshua all his life, but only distantly. The old man had lived in the little town when Satchel was a child, but he had moved his practice and his home closer to the big town when the highway severed the small town from passing traffic. The vet had had, some years earlier, a tremendous argument with William, for Joshua was a strict nonbeliever and William's ideology had, one day, trampled on what the veterinarian saw as his own ground. Claiming in the pub that God would provide for His people as surely as He provided for the birds in the sky and the lambs in the fields, William had been confronted with the irate old man who listed all the cases he could remember of lambs and birds whom the Almighty seemed to have overlooked. The incident had irreparably soured the men's opinion of each other, but the vet never extended his contempt for the father to the son, or to Satchel's mother. He did, in fact, feel it his duty to tell them, and anyone who would listen, that he felt for them greatly.

He put his palms on the table and straightened himself, wincing at the burning of the arthritis in his spine. "The blood," he said shortly, "it's nothing to worry about. She's cut her tongue, that's all. A few stitches will fix it. I won't know the full extent of the damage to her leg until I can x-ray her in the surgery. She's in shock, but not too deeply. It's her breathing that concerns me. See this?"

Satchel stepped nearer, and the vet pressed his hands to Moke's ribs. When he spoke, Satchel could smell the sweetness of cigars in his words. "When she breathes in, her abdomen doesn't expand. It collapses, as if she were breathing out. When she does breathe out, her abdomen expands. She's doing exactly the opposite to what is normal. She's ruptured her diaphragm."

Satchel looked at him blankly. "Can it be fixed?"

"It can. Her leg—I can feel pieces of bone floating around in there, and we might get away with pinning it, but my guess is it will need plating. That will be fiddly, but far from impossible."

"So you can save her?"

Joshua went to the sink and washed his hands. "I could try," he replied. "I could do my best. Her injury is survivable. But I couldn't promise anything. She'll need a big operation, and that is traumatic for an animal. I am not a miracle man, Satchel, but I would do for her the best I could."

Satchel nodded. "All right," he said, "I'll help you carry her to the car—"

"No," said Joshua, "wait. Sit down, Satchel, and listen to me."

Satchel hesitated, but when Joshua drew a chair out

from under the counter, he sat in it obediently. The vet went to the fridge and poured a glass of milk, passing it to Satchel reverently, as though it was a potion. Then he leaned against the sink and crossed his arms. In the light coming through the window, Satchel could see downy hair scattered over his face, as if what had fallen from his scalp over the years had implanted itself in his cheeks and nose.

"Your dog has sustained serious injuries," Joshua began. "But, as I say, all things going well, it's not beyond repair. What it will be, however, is expensive."

Satchel sagged, the glass hovering near his lips. "How much?"

"I would estimate a couple of thousand dollars. Maybe a bit less, if her leg is not too bad."

Satchel felt as though his blood had been suctioned and his veins refilled with air. "I don't have that much money," he said.

"I know. Not many people around here do. And I know your family has been doing it hard for a number of years."

"Isn't there anything—isn't there some other way?"

Joshua's face creased. "You could get your father to pray for help," he suggested, "or you could have her put to sleep."

Satchel stood up quickly. Moke was lying peacefully, and the blood had stopped seeping from her mouth. He ran a hand along her body, and she made a halfhearted effort to get up. He eased her down again, smoothing back her satin ears. "She's my friend," he said. "I want her to live."

Joshua nodded. "People become very attached to their animals. But sometimes there's nothing we can do. Sometimes, our alternatives are all as hopeless as each other. I can keep her comfortable overnight, if you want time to think about it."

Satchel said nothing. He looked into Moke's eyes. He could hardly remember a time when those glittering orbs hadn't followed him closely, accompanying everything he did. When he looked at her, he hardly registered that what he saw was dog: she was his ever-present shadow. Hers was the face he saw on waking: she was the one who wanted to be with him, the one who watched and waited for him, who felt his absence badly. She was a clown when he needed cheering, the ears for his thoughts and plans. She had given him reason to get up in the morning, and she had stopped the days from seeming too long. He looked at her, and he thought. He thought about money, how it had strangled his life bloodless for so many years. His mother had once told him not to think about money and to see, instead, all the good things he had. She had given him a puppy, and he suddenly felt that Moke was the only purely good thing he had ever known.

"Joshua," he said, "if I could get the money in a few months, would you fix her now?"

"Where would you get those sort of funds, Satchel?"

He kept his hands on Moke's cool body. He thought he'd have to drag the words from himself but they came with surprising ease. "I have a friend who's offered me a job. I'd have to go a long way from here, but I could send you money every week. It would take a while, but I'd pay you back eventually."

Joshua lowered his eyes, considering. Satchel waited, tensing with dread. He did not know what he would do if the vet refused and he prayed that the old man, like Laura, could look beyond money and see something more. If he couldn't, Satchel wondered where he would search to find worth in anything. There would be no point, anymore, in trying to live decently, in being good in the hope that this would bring goodness.

Joshua finally looked at him, and thumped the sink with a hand. "I'm a soft bloody touch," he said. "You better keep your promise, young man, or I'll be after you with a hatchet. Animals I like; people I don't trust or care for. I'll fix your friend, but I'll have my eye on you."

Satchel helped him carry the dog to the car, and when the vet had driven off with her and left him alone in the shade of the school bus, he sank against a tire and calmed himself until he was sure he would not cry.

160

He drove the bus around the outskirts of the big town, hoping the huge silver vehicle would go unseen. He felt lonely without Moke beside him and he was wretched with concern for her, but he tried to put her from his mind. He had told her to be a good dog and knew she would try to be.

He parked the bus on the side of the road where Gosling wouldn't see it and walked the remaining distance to the foreman's home. Gosling's house was prim and tidy and seemed anxious with the strain of being eternally on its best behavior. He must have seen Satchel walking up the driveway, because he came out to the porch wearing his dressing gown and slippers, a stub-faced toddler lolling in his arms. "O'Rye?" he called. "What brings you here, at this time of the morning?"

Satchel stopped in the garden, hugging his coat around himself. "I've been thinking about that job with your brother-in-law, Gos. I'd like to take it, if I can."

The baby was gumming a corner of her bib, and Gosling pried the material from her grip, grinning and cooing at the child, but the face he turned to Satchel was solemn. "Mrs. Gosling was speaking to Tom a couple of nights ago. Apparently he's already got someone in mind for the job. He got tired of waiting to hear an answer from me. I'm sorry, Satch—I should have told you."

Satchel felt as though the ground had rippled beneath his feet. "No," he said, "he can't do that. I've got to have that job, Gosling—"

"And I wanted you to have it, Satchel. But what could I say? A man can't wait forever when he's got work to be done."

Satchel glanced helplessly around the garden. Mrs. Gosling grew fuchsias in the fashion that he hated, the foliage posted high on one thin brown stick. He couldn't think of anything to say, and he knew that if he did speak, his voice would be high as a bell, taut as a wire. The baby gurgled wetly, and Gosling jiggled her in his arms. "Has something happened, Satchel?" he asked.

Satchel looked down at the grass. His boots were soaked, and he wondered distantly when they had become so. Water made his vision murky, and he blinked it away. He heard the foreman ask if anything had happened to Laura, and shook his head mutely. "What, then?" Gosling demanded.

Satchel sniffed, and lifted his head. "Nothing," he said. "I just needed that job, that's all."

Gosling regarded him, rocking the toddler absently. "I suppose I could phone Tom," he mused, "find out what plans he's made. Mrs. Gosling might have got her story a bit fuddled. Tom's a busy kind of bloke — he might not have got around to actually doing much. Might be thinking, not doing. Come inside and I'll give him a ring."

Satchel stepped onto the veranda and hooked off his shoes. Everything was as neat and sparkling inside the house as it was on the outside, and Mrs. Gosling had rules that kept it that way. There was no sign anywhere of the children who lived here, no toys or scuffs on the walls. A woman who kept house so strictly, thought Satchel, was not the sort to get her story fuddled.

Gosling lowered the baby onto a rug in the lounge room and tickled her many chins. "It's just me and Annabella at home these days," he told Satchel. "Mrs. Gosling goes to the shop and the kiddies go to school, and me and bubby have to take care of ourselves. Don't we, bubba? Yeah, we do. You and your fat old dad."

Satchel watched the baby pawing at its toes while

Gosling went into the hall to make the telephone call. He wasn't thinking anything, and his mind felt smogged and empty. When the child twisted and made to slap the hot bars of the heater, it took him a moment to unlock his mouth and say, "No."

The baby looked at him, her eyes a deep blue, lashy inheritance from her father.

Gosling returned, his brows drawn together. "Not answering," he sighed. "Not home."

Satchel nodded: it seemed a result he'd expected. "Thanks for trying, anyway," he said. "I'd better go."

"No, you wait." Gosling shifted the toddler from her place near the heater, the child keeping her legs straight out before her while she moved through the air. The foreman sat on the couch and put his hands on his thighs, eyeing Satchel intently. "Something's happened—I can see that. You don't have to tell me what it is. You need money, do you? Or you need to get away from here? One or the other."

Satchel shuffled his feet. The heater was roaring, scorching the back of his jeans. Gosling leaned into the couch and pondered the ceiling. "I'll tell you what I'll do," he said. "I'll ring Tom tonight and find out what he's up to. If he's got someone else in mind, if he's already got the job fixed up, there's not much I can say. It's not fair to chuck a man out of work he's already

been promised. If, on the other hand, he hasn't promised anyone anything, I'll tell him that you're ready
whenever he is. All right?"

"Yes."

"I'll tell him you can be packed and on your way
within the next couple of days. Can you do that?"

"Sure."

Gosling looked sideways at him. "You promise me,
O'Rye?"

Satchel nodded jerkily, and Gosling hefted himself
to his feet. "Good," he said. "I'll do my best. Now, cup
of tea?"

"No. Thanks, Gos. I have to go."

Gosling ambled after him down the hall. "You ring
me tonight," he instructed, "after eight. I should have
spoken to Tom by then."

"All right."

Gosling held the door open but stood, for a
moment, blocking Satchel's way. "You're not in trouble,
are you?" he asked. "You haven't done something you
shouldn't have done, have you?"

Satchel smiled. "Kind of."

Gosling shook his head sadly. "Well, you need me,
you know where I am. We'll go on the run together.
You and me and Annabella."

"I'll speak to you tonight. Thanks again, Gos."

"Yeah," said Gosling, "that's my pleasure. Take care."

Satchel waved when he reached the front gate, and the foreman raised a hand in saluting reply.

He sat at the wheel of the bus and wondered where he should go. He supposed people were looking for him by now, determined to retrieve their bus. He smiled blackly to think of what they would say to each other: the men in the O'Rye family could obviously not be trusted around school transport. His mother, he knew, would be cross at him. She hated theft, and Satchel had stolen the bus. He could take it back, park it in the schoolyard and slink stealthily away, but that would leave him with no means of getting home except to walk, or catch the passenger bus. He was not in the mood to wait at the stop, shivering and exhausted, wrung with fretfulness. He started the engine and headed home the way he had come, keeping to the quietest streets until he turned onto the old road and the countryside opened around him, vacant as a desert.

He parked the bus outside Chelsea's house, trusting she would know what to do with it, and walked to the main street. It was just over two hours since he had left his home and not all the shops had opened for the day, but Timothy's Take-Away rolled up its shutters at dawn and Satchel ducked through its doors. He wasn't hungry or thirsty, but when Timothy looked at him expectantly, he ordered a toasted sandwich and took a seat at the table. It was cold inside the store because Timothy begrudged the expense of heating, and Satchel clasped his hands between his knees. If word had traveled about his theft of the bus, Timothy would surely know of it and have something to say, but he said nothing, his birdlike back turned to Satchel as he grilled two pieces of bread. Satchel bowed his head and closed his eyes.

The buzz of the alarm at the door made him open them again and he saw Boxer Piper cross the floor, yank open the refrigerator, and take from the shelves a carton of milk. He said with authority to Timothy, "And a packet of Winny Reds."

Timothy scarcely glanced at the boy. Boxer waited, but the shopkeeper did not snake a hand into the cigarette shelves, and finally Boxer kicked the counter peevishly, dumping from his fist a scattering of coins. He whirled, and spied Satchel. "Hey," he chirped. "Heard about the bus, Satchy. Cool. That was so cool."

He propped opposite Satchel and wiped away strands of his coppery hair. Boxer was twelve, and precocious. "All those kids are going to think you're a legend, nicking the school bus. You shouldn't have brought it back — you should have just kept driving and driving."

"Hmm," said Satchel. "Shouldn't you be at school?"

"Hate school. Not going anymore. How's the mutt?"

"OK."

"Huh. Must be shitty, running over your own dog. Have you got a cigarette?"

"No."

Boxer pouted. Timothy stalked to the table with the steaming sandwich on a plate and waited for Satchel to find some money. He could not find enough, and the shopkeeper's face wrinkled. "You can pay the rest next time you come in," he said.

"You maggot!" squawked Boxer. "You're a prick, you are! How many years has Satchel been coming in here and buying your crappy food and you're worrying about a few cents! I'm gonna open a shop one day and send you out of business."

Timothy sneered. "You're never going to do anything. You're a waste of space."

Boxer held up a finger and Timothy glared at it malevolently, evidently tempted to snap the digit from the boy's hand. Then he turned and creaked to the kitchen, disappearing beyond the fly-screen strapping. Boxer grinned at Satchel. "We could piss in the deep fryer," he said, "but I think he does that already."

Satchel passed him a triangle of sandwich, and the boy demolished it rapidly in wide famished bites, his cheeks bulging like a squirrel's. The toast left a mustache of crumbs on his lip and he stuck out his tongue and brushed them onto it. Satchel asked, "Have you heard from Leroy?"

"Yeah, he phoned a couple of days ago." Boxer found a lump of cheese congealing under a nail and nibbled at it with teeth too large for his head. "Says he's got a girl-friend, but I don't believe him. He's just making it up. Chelsea believes him, though. Says Leroy's voice was all gooey, so it must be true. Not that she'd know anything about girlfriends and boyfriends, but."

"You shouldn't be mean about your sister," said Satchel.

"Why not?"

"Because she's your sister. And she never says any-thing mean about you."

"That's because I'm so cool," said Boxer.

Satchel dusted his hands over the plate. The toast had stuck in Boxer's throat, and he coughed raucously, pounding his ribs. Recovered, he asked, "So what are you gonna do now?"

"Go home."

"Wouldn't do that if I were you. The cops might have staked your place out. You know what I reckon you should do? You should wait at the tracks and jump a train. I've been thinking about doing that. I've got it all planned out; I know the best spot to jump from. I'll show you, if you want."

Satchel smiled. He rested his chin in his hands. His mind seemed to be swimming through a quagmire strewn with metallic debris, and he felt tired enough to lie down and sleep, right there at the table. Boxer waited for a reply to his offer and, getting none, pushed out his chair and hefted the milk carton. "If you need me," he said, "you know where I am. I'll see you later, Satchy."

He went, the milk bumping against his beanpole legs. Satchel sat alone for some minutes more, struggling against drowsiness. When Timothy came out to see what was happening, Satchel took his plate to the counter and shambled into the glare of the morning. He took the route he knew well enough to walk with his eyes closed: past the shops, past the houses, past clumps of fenced untended land and then, when he reached the sign that had once advertised the service station, cutting diagonally across the concrete yard and up the front steps of his home.

He was aware, immediately, of raised voices and a tightness to the air, as if the voices required more oxygen than the house could hold. He paused in the shadows of the hallway, sure the shouting was the end result of all that had happened to him that morning and knowing he could delay his fate, if he wanted, that he could sneak away easily and they would never know he had been here. He listened while he hesitated, and heard none of the words he expected to hear. It dawned on him what was happening and he was suddenly running.

The young electrician Jamie was bailed up against a kitchen wall. His washed-out eyes were bulging, and his arms were raised defensively. William was storming back and forth in front of him, shouting, his voice throttled with rage. Laura was plucking at her husband's sleeve, and the words she was using to distract his attention were tripping from her frantically.

Satchel ducked past her and squared a hand against his father's chest, forcing him away from Jamie. The electrician leaped sideways, the same movement mice make in a moment of freedom from the claws of a cat. "Dad!" Satchel cried. "What are you doing?"

"Don't talk to me, Judas!" William bellowed back at him. "You traitor! You reprobate! How dare you ask payment for the things I do!"

Satchel closed his fingers in his father's shirt, keeping his elbow locked and William effectively pinned. He glanced at Jamie, who was scuffling backward to the kitchen door. Seen by Satchel, the electrician blurted, "I thought you were joking. I thought you were — joking —"

"Go," said Satchel. "Go, now."

And Jamie went, in a streak of garish flannel, the screen door banging shut after him. Satchel turned to his father, who was not struggling. Laura, too, was standing still, a hand pressed to her mouth. Satchel's heart was pounding, and for a moment the kitchen was quiet enough for him to imagine he could hear it thud tautly in his chest. Then, "Have you finished?" William asked frostily.

"Calm down, Dad—"

"I am calm. You can see I am extremely calm. While I am pinioned by Judas's hand at my throat, what else could I be?"

Satchel released his grip, and William straightened his snarled shirt. Satchel looked at his mother, who was blinking at the floor. There was money wafting over the boards, a blue note trapped under William's boot. "Let me tell you what happened here this morning," said William, and Satchel let him, although he already knew. "That young man, whom you have just seen flee, came knocking on our door some ten to fifteen minutes ago, wanting to pay me for repairing his father's generator. I told him that I do not accept money for what I do willingly, but he claimed my son told him that, contrary to what I believe, I am always paid for the good work I do. He said my son joked that the money should be paid straight to himself, so he might go to a hotel and use it to buy alcohol. But the young man thought it best if I received the money directly, as it was I who repaired the generator."

Satchel only looked at him, and Laura said nothing

either, but William said, "Please don't try to deny it. Please do not insult my intelligence by denying what is cruelly obvious to me. My son has been taking money for what I do. You have betrayed my promise to God. I have kept the ways of the Lord, and have not wickedly departed from my God, and you, a devil, have made mockery of His kindness. You have prostituted me. You have sold my soul."

"It's not Satchel who's—"

"Mum, don't, be quiet—"

"No," snapped Laura, jerking up her head, "I will not be quiet. Satchel is not the one who has taken money for your work, William. It was me: people pay me for what you do. I've been given the money, and what little there is of it I've used to buy food for you, and clothes, and to pay for the water you drink, for the electricity you use, for the petrol to drive you to church. I pay for your paintbrushes, for your haircuts, for your bootlaces, for your newspapers, for everything you prefer to believe has simply fallen from the sky. God hasn't provided any of those things, William. *I've* provided them—I can remember writing the checks. I can remember asking shopkeepers to give me just one more week to find the money, just one more day. I've kept you alive and clean and fed, William, for years. I don't know what God has been doing all that time, but He certainly hasn't been taking much notice of you."

William watched as she got to her knees and began collecting the money, crunching each note in her hand. "Traitors," he muttered. "Lord, hear me in my trouble. The Lord my God will enlighten my darkness. The Lord is my rock, my fortress, and my deliverer. Hear me, Lord, for I am surrounded on all sides by traitors."

"Yes, no doubt you are. But we need the money."

"My God, help me. For dogs have compassed me: the assembly of the wicked have enclosed me, they pierced my hands and my feet—"

Laura clicked her tongue impatiently. "Stop it," she growled. "Just stop it, William. Go to your room and quieten down."

"I'll pray for you."

"I don't want you to pray for me. Your prayers don't go anywhere. They don't do anything."

William gasped: he made a move toward his kneeling wife, but Satchel grabbed him, and spun him. For the smallest splinter of time father and son looked into each other's eyes and Satchel saw that William was not angry, but damaged, and drifting, and old. He let his fist go through the air anyway, let it take with it all the distress that had collected in him that day and all the fury and frustration that had kindled in him over years. He hit his father as hard as he could, wishing he could hit harder, wishing he could hurt his father so much that the pain would never ease, that he would feel it every waking and sleeping moment for all his days that remained. It was a terrible satisfaction, to feel his knuckles collide with William's skull.

His father dropped to the floor and rolled sideways, bumping against a leg of the table and curling around it like a worm. Blood was spurting from his nose and was smearing his neck and chin. Satchel's hand smarted, but the satisfaction he felt was suddenly not enough: engulfed in resentment and pleased by the sight of what he could do and wondering why he hadn't done so years ago, he might have reached for William's collar if Laura hadn't shouted, "Satchel!"

She shepherded her son away from her husband, and Satchel could see she was outraged: she batted at his face and shoulders and he dodged clear of her flailing arms. "What did you do that for?" she screeched. "You tell me, Satchel, why you would do such a thing!"

Satchel stumbled, and lied. "He was going to hurt you—"

"When has he ever hurt me? You go outside! Go on, out of my sight! My God, Satchel, what do you think you've achieved? Out! Out!"

He let her push him to the doorway and through it, and he watched her grab a tea towel from the rail and press it into William's face. William was moaning and sliding his limbs about the floor. She garbled comforting words to him and, catching sight of her son, hissed, "Go, I told you. Go and cool down. I'm very angry with you, Satchel."

He stepped off the side of the veranda and stood staring across the yard; the chickens were still caged in their coop, and he went over to open the gate for them. They trundled past his ankles and waddled briskly to the orchard, to pluck from the soft earth there the shoots that had broken through overnight. Then he walked down the driveway, past the house and the petrol pumps and the big, worn-out, pointless service-station sign, and headed into town.

In the main street he passed people who smiled and nodded at him, who stopped in the expectation that he would stop too, as he usually would do, and gazed after him in surprise when he kept up his pace. No one mentioned the school bus, and if they had done so, he would not have cared. He wouldn't have bothered to explain. He walked on, past Timothy like a raven in his doorway and past the board outside the firehouse that judged the likelihood of bushfire to be low. He kept walking, never veering from the shoulder of the road, past the signpost to the cemetery and through the shade of the mill, and soon his coat became too hot for him, but he did not stop to take it off. Banks of gravel crumbled under his feet and made him slide; he stepped over solid waves of mud sloughed up by careering cars. A van slowed alongside him, and he shook his head at the raised eyebrows of the driver, for he did not want a ride.

When he arrived at the station wagon, he saw the key was still in the ignition and that the back seat, where Moke had been, was stained with browning blood. He sat behind the steering wheel and tried the key, but the engine merely grizzled and he let it go silent. He thought about leaving his coat in the car, but the weather had been changeable lately and if it started to rain, he would need the coat's protection, be grateful for its warmth and bulk. He had no idea how long his mother intended him to stay away, but he would go home only when he decided to. He might not wait until her mood was better and William's nose had been snuffled clean, or he might wait much longer than that. He took the keys, locked up the wagon, and resumed his journey.

He had never walked the unmarked track to the mountain, and when he did so, he saw things he never noticed from the car — small forests of green-hood orchids, the flattened and tatty corpse of a possum, midges swarming the air above a cloudy pungent puddle, brick-red mushrooms of tuft fungus growing at the base of trees, clustered as if for a family portrait. He saw tire patterns preserved in the sun-dried mud and recognized them as belonging to the wagon. He touched them with the toe of his boot and they disintegrated easily.

It took over an hour to reach the clearing, and when he got there, he lay down on a flat shelf of the mountain, tucked his feet beneath his coat and a hand against his face, and was asleep as soon as his eyes were closed.

He woke into blazing daylight and pushed himself up on one arm, fumbling to remember who he was and where he was and what he might be doing. His movement spooked a flock of scarlet-beaked finches from the depths of the grass and they twirled into the sky, piping fractiously. His eyes followed them as they dispersed into the trees; he thought he had heard their cheeping in his dreams but could no longer remember having slept. His head hurt, and his bones were sore where they had pressed against the volcano. He was hungry, and the knuckles that had connected with the ridge of William's eye socket were reluctant to move.

*   *   *

He sat up and dangled his legs over the edge of the shelving. The sun was at the peak of its low-slung winter ellipse, and he knew he must have slept for a couple of hours. He flopped down again, hoping he might go back to sleep, but his eyes would not stay shut and blinked open at the slightest sound, finally roaming the clearing of their own free will. He sighed, and got to his feet. The red gums creaked as a breeze rushed through them, but to Satchel it sounded as if they had made a bet among themselves that had just been won: he could not stay as still as they, having one place on the earth was not enough for him. He bundled his coat into a ball and crammed it into the rock, jumped from the shelf and began to walk the base of the volcano. When he found a place that seemed to offer purchase for his fingers and furrows for his toes, he began to climb.

Satchel had climbed the mountain before, but not very often. He saw the mountain every day, and because he had been born and reared in its overhang, it had never been a thing of great interest or attraction to him. He had a couple of cousins, and when they were young they had been sent here for a holiday and he had climbed the mountain with them, keeping to the tame and painted tourist path. He had been alarmed and rather thrilled when one of them had gazed down at the dot that was her family's car and, realizing how far she had come, begun to thrash and howl. She'd been carried to the ground by William, where she collapsed in a huddle and dug her nails into the dirt. Now Satchel chose a route that was unmarked and had possibly never been climbed before, and he expected the mountain to throw him off at any moment, shaking him away like a beast that feels the feet of a fly tickling a sensitive spot. He would not be angry if that happened: he would return to the ground and find another beginning and start the climb over. He told the volcano that he had nothing better to do, that he had the afternoon to reach the summit and that he had patience, he would not be easily deterred. He climbed, hedging one foot past the other, stretching his arms and exploring the region above his head with his fingertips. The rock was cold when it touched him, and water was pooled in pockmarks on its hide. Sometimes, not often, serious climbers came to the mountain, bringing with them pulleys and colorful expensive ropes. They chose routes they judged intractable. They hammered pikes into fissures, and the tinny clink of metal upon metal could be heard for miles, if the climber had climbed high enough. A climber had fallen once, years ago. His expensive ropes had not saved him, and he'd fallen like a bird dropped dead in the sky. He had been an old man who looked younger when he returned to earth.

Satchel paused to breathe, his feet wobbling on a quiver of stone. He pressed an ear against the rock, fancying to think there would be something to hear. There were caves in the mountain and most of them quickly narrowed impassably, but a torch shone through the gap sometimes lit up huge caverns beyond, and tunnels and caves beyond these. Something very small and lithe might make it through those tunnels, something that thrived in a darkness as thick as space, but Satchel heard nothing, no rustling, nothing to say he wasn't absolutely alone. He looked down at the drop below him: he was high enough to hurt himself if he fell, and he could not see the dents in the rock that had let him come so far. He scratched his forehead against the mountain and probed for a foothold.

Eventually he came to a place that was sloped enough to let him sit and rest, his knees pulled up tight in front of him to prevent him from sliding. He did not let himself look at the scenery: he wanted to see it from the top. Instead he looked at where he was going and saw the mountain was bunched and jumbled, a rocky jigsaw that had been mangled in a temper. Great knobby broods of hardened lava reared from the surface, and moss, oozing liquid, was plastered in their shadows. Here and there were thin outposts of greenery, weeds that had fallen here as seeds and landed, with luck, in pockets of topsoil blown in from the farmlands. The rest of his climb would be easier and Satchel was disappointed, but he saw he had a long way to go yet and this was pleasing. He pushed his sleeves above his elbows and rested for a few minutes more.

He reached the summit on his hands and soaked knees, the slant of the volcano forcing him into the humbled position. His jeans were scraped and his palms were burning, and at one point he had paused to take off his shirt and let it flutter down the side of the mountain. He had thought, too late, of the danger of having it snag in the canopy of a tree, but it did not do so: it drifted against the rock and tumbled airily to the ground, landing in a pile in the grass. He wore, now, a ragged T-shirt that changed color as his skin dampened, for the afternoon was warm and heat was attracted to the volcano, which sucked it in like a lizard or a snake. Once he actually saw a lizard, a dart of quicksilver that dashed from his path and, out of reach, craned its head to look at him, its flesh pulsing in the dip behind its forelegs. Then it flashed away, disappearing completely although there was nothing that might hide it, no slit or convenient hollow. It vanished, a magician.

At the summit he sprawled on his back, staring for a time at the blueness of the sky. He looked at the sun and felt its hypnotic lull, averting his eyes before it could capture and sear them. He spread his arms wide, his fingers bending from the mountain's surface, and allowed himself to recover. He would have liked to sleep here, in this safe lonely place on top of his world, but he was no longer tired, he couldn't even yawn.

He sat up and studied all he could see laid before him, the scrub that surrounded the base of the mountain, the fields that eased up and fell gently as they made their way closer to the mass as if the mountain stood surrounded by a worshiping, undulating crowd. The mountain was a benign ruler now, but what a different landscape it must have been when the volcano was active, a scorching despot that drooled fire when it spoke, and spat blazingly. The crowd would have cringed; the air must have shaken with the roaring, crashing, rivening sound of the tyrant's eruptions, and rubble would have rained on everything for miles around, rocks slamming craters out of the earth, trees smashing and exploding. Apart from the occasional boulder standing inexplicably in a paddock, it was difficult, now, to see any remnant of those lawless days.

Satchel got to his feet and could see farther: he could trace the dark slash of the old road all the way to his town. He could see the green arena of the cricket ground and the spire of the wooden church, and he could see the roofs of some shops. They were tiny from here, smaller than his smallest fingernail. A meek, faltering little town, with no reason to exist anymore, hated more and more deeply by each new generation born into it, a town that didn't need a name and one day would not have one. It was waiting for people to move on, to give up on it, or to die. It would not, then, become a ghost town, because its buildings would be soon pulled down. Already there was talk of demolishing the flour mills, for no apparent reason.

He turned and began walking, his hands ready to save him if he tripped on the uncertain surface. The summit of the volcano was huge, a landscape in itself. Small mountains sprouted here, and arched bridges of stone. There were niches and alcoves and gullies deep enough to climb into, and there were channels that became rivers in the rain. From no point on the summit could a far edge be seen: one had to choose a direction and take it, without knowing when the perimeter would again be met. Everything but the moss was gray, or some shade of sooty black; when the summer sun came and scorched this place, the moss would soon match its surroundings, turning brown and scabby and finally gray before crumbling and blowing away.

All day he had refused to think about what had been happening to him, refusing to think while events rearranged his existence before his eyes, but he felt calmer now, safer in the refuge that the mountain's crown allowed. If he stayed here, with the breeze tossing his hair and flicking the hem of his T-shirt, nothing more could happen to him, and no one would come to speak to him. Satchel sat down, splaying his legs in front of him, and leaned back on his arms.

Whatever Moke needed doing would have been done to her by now, and he hoped she was sleeping soundly, the blood cleaned away from her, Joshua's vigilant eyes on the rightened rise and fall of her chest. Satchel would not consider the chance that she had not survived the operation: she was strong and healthy, and she wanted to live. He knew she was alive — he would feel it if things were otherwise; he would hear it in the wind and sense it in his bones. She was alive, and he missed her. She seemed to have been gone a long time. She was a naughty dog and she had changed his life now, twice.

He plucked away a strand of hair that had swept into his mouth, and hunched forward, shielding his face from the wind. The rock had left images of itself in his palms and he rubbed his hands together but the indented impressions remained. By tomorrow he would know if Gosling had secured the job for him, and Satchel did not know what he was going to do if the big foreman had failed. He did not know what he would tell Joshua, how he could explain the things that had happened to him, how exactly his intentions had gone wrong. And if Gosling had managed to get him the job,

Satchel would be gone from here in a few days, traveling up the coast into a land of cyclones and sea and the overweight weather of the tropics. Laura would be happy, Leroy would be envious, and Gosling would be proud, but the thought made Satchel queasy. He would be going to a place of strangers; he'd know no one he passed on the streets. The ocean would surround him, and water was not a thing he knew. He rolled a stone beneath his boot, rattling it across the bumpy surface, thinking. It seemed suddenly clear that Laura and William had incarcerated him in this place, as everyone had warned him they would do. Laura spoke to him of escaping and let him think he stayed because he wanted to, but all the while she had been drawing the bars around him tighter, and now he was wary of strangers and vexed by thoughts of elsewhere.

He was glad he had hit William, and that this had horrified Laura. He didn't care what William said to him when he went home. He would look askance at his father's puffy face and there would be silence then. There had been a second, back there in the kitchen, when Satchel had genuinely believed that William was moving with violence toward Laura, but that second had passed, and Satchel had seen he was wrong. He'd hit his father anyway, and he wasn't sorry. Laura could say whatever she liked, but William had deserved it. He'd been asking for it for years. If Gosling got the job for him, Satchel would pack and leave gladly. He would do the job he had to do and then he would buy himself a fishing boat, spend his days on the waves. Moke would be there: he'd have her put on a train and sent up to him because he wasn't coming back himself, once he'd finally got away. He'd have Moke and a boat and the ocean, and when mountains rose before him then, they would take the shape of whales.

Satchel sniffed and rubbed his eyes. The breeze was making them water, and making his nose run. For a moment he had felt powerful in anger, but the feeling drained out of him, leaving him slump-shouldered with a mute throbbing pain behind the eyes. He tossed his head defiantly, but still he felt ship-wrecked. There would be hours of daylight before this day ended.

The day crawled. He wondered if anyone else was feeling the sluggishness of time. He thought about going to the tame side of the mountain and watching any tourists there, but the idea seemed somehow pathetic. The information building had tables where visitors could have coffee and he was passingly tempted to go there, somewhere out of the wind, but he would make a curious sight for the tourists, dirty and sweaty as he was, and the lady who ran the place would soon harry him away. He could go, instead, to Gosling's house, but

Gosling would ask him questions and Satchel was in no mood for the unrelenting domesticity that encircled the foreman. He could go to see Chelsea, who would not ask him anything—rather, Satchel would be forced to do the talking, wringing out his anxiety to the person least able to help him, and end up feeling like a fool. And so he chose to do none of these things, resigning himself to staying alone.

He climbed down the mountain on one of the easier slopes and had to walk for a long time before he arrived where he'd begun and found his shirt rumpled in the grass. He shook it out and slipped it on and kept walking until he reached the shelf where he'd left his coat. He folded it into a pillow and stretched out on the ledge. The clearing was pinging with the sound of bell-birds talking to each other, and he tried to search them out but could not find them. He never found them: he had no idea what a bellbird actually looked like. The sky had grown dimmer, and the sun was smothered behind a battalion of cloud. It was late in the afternoon, he guessed, and much cooler now. Satchel wriggled until he was as comfortable as the ledge was going to let him be, and closed his eyes. When he opened them again it was early evening and mosquitoes were biting his wrist.

He jumped from the ledge and tramped into the clearing, shrugging on his coat as he went and turning up its collar. Bark and leaves broke crisply beneath him every time he set a foot down. He was not going home until the night was black and the stars were out, but already the moon was there, an opaque white sphere set into an ashen sky. He was hungry, and his stomach made a mournful, complaining noise.

The red gums around the clearing were empty because birds didn't roost here, they simply passed through, and it was quiet enough to hear the shuffle of his coat against his calves. When he stopped and listened carefully, he heard the zoom of a vehicle on the highway, and it was the only thing that spoiled the feeling that civilization had ended while he slept and his was the only history left to record. He smiled at the thought of how much easier that would make it for him to greet the following morning.

What rebelliousness he had talked into himself at the peak of the mountain was gone, and carved out in its place was an echoing sense of misery. Satchel had refused, all his life, to feel sorry for himself, and he mostly believed he had nothing to feel sorry about, but his life now seemed devastated by the happenings of a sole, endless, catastrophic day. It amazed him to realize how precarious his happiness must have been, that a handful of events, strung together almost randomly, could raze it to the ground. When he came to the chopping stump, he pressed his fingers into the gouges left by the chain saw and thought about his past differently: if he tried, he could fit together the pieces that linked everything into a train that led from this moment, standing here, to that moment, weeks ago, when the chain saw had juddered in his grip and chips of wood had gone flying. Maybe nothing was ever random, and maybe, if he tried harder, he could link into the train every minute of his life, all of them leading in the one direction that found him standing in the clearing and shrinking from his future. He rubbed his face and sat down alongside the cracked relic of the long-vanished tree. The tree had been gone for longer than Satchel had been alive, but it must have stood for hundreds of years before that, because the stump it left was massive, as broad as a table. Once it had been respectable to slay a mighty tree, and he wondered if it was under this bravado that the red gum met its fate or if it had been cut for its own good, before it toppled and brought down with it an acre of its children.

He curled against the stump and tucked the coat around his knees, hoping the dampness of the earth would not seep through it too quickly. The wind was blowing tempestuously, a constant buffeting on his face that chilled his lips and the blunted tip of his nose and threw his hair about roughly so it snagged on the bark and slapped at his eyes. He wanted to go home, but the thought of being there made him wonder why he imagined it would be better than being here. He could hardly bear to think of meeting William, of seeing his battered face. William was his father, and he was only ill. He had tried to be a good man, and he had always loved Satchel. But everything in the past was now tainted by what Satchel had done, and everything in the future would happen in its shadow. William would not be the same father, and Satchel could never be the same son. He remembered a time, years ago, when he'd been helping William string wire fencing: he had let the wire go, knowing it would whiplash backward and strike his father, but he hadn't really meant it to happen; he hadn't meant the result to be so *real*. William had bled terribly, but although he knew Satchel had done what he did deliberately, having seen a shimmer of mischief in his eyes, he had never been angry at his son, or disappointed. Perhaps he understood that boys were naturally bad sometimes, unable to help themselves. This time, things would be different. William might forgive him, but things were going to change. From now on he would see himself differently in the reflection of Satchel's eyes.

And Satchel had always tried to be a good son, waging the war of a lifetime against a hard little stone of malignancy that refused to accept his father's sickness, refused to forgive or feel compassion for him. But it had had the upper hand when the moment finally came: Satchel had hit William not because he had to, but because he'd wanted to. He had enjoyed it, and would have done it again. When the time came, it hadn't even been a contest.

A bird cut through the space above him, a sharp pointed arrowhead rushing the air toward the mountain. It flew fast, as if it had been forgotten by its brothers and was desperate to rejoin the flock. But mountain birds as big as that were rarely flocking birds, unless they were ducks or swans: large birds were preying birds, and this one was chasing something that

Satchel had not seen. He lowered his chin behind the edge of his collar, squinting into the iciness of the wind. He would miss the mountain if he went away, although the mountain was not something he thought about often, and when he did so, it was sometimes with aggravation, as though the mountain stood in his way. Still, he would miss it. It had closed him in, but it had also been protective, a massive gargoyle at the gates of his world. There were no gates at the ocean: when you looked toward it, you didn't see anything. All that water gave you no sense of how far you needed to go before you finally got somewhere. He would be alone there, and things would be strange to him.

And if he didn't go—if he couldn't go—if he'd lost the chance to go because he'd delayed and delayed his decision, his feet sunk immobile in the earth, the situation would not be easier, but worse. He would be haunted by a debt he was unable to pay, and Laura would feel compelled to help him. She would take more shifts at the geriatric home, and her hands would crack and peel and crack deeper again: he would hear her quiet winces of pain and know who was to blame. And he would see William every day, eternally.

He huddled on the ground, groaning softly, mud clinging to the hand he put down. The wind was freezing and making him feel scoured. He tightened his body into the smallest, warmest shape it would go. His mind was running around a circle, and the constant spin of it was leaving him nauseous. He did not for one second wish he could rewind time and start the day over — he was not a dreamer. What he did do was shut his eyes against the gathering gloom and pray to God to find a way out for him, to let him stumble upon a trap-door he had not yet noticed that would give him an answer, a solution, an alternative he had overlooked so far. He prayed to the God of his mother, who was merciful and pitying, and he prayed to the God of his father, who commanded thunderbolts and could twist the world off its axis. He pleaded for escape from the whirling of his mind, from the fear and desperation that were shrilling around after it. Give me another way, he prayed: *provide*.

A whisper in the grass made him flip his eyes open and he stared, not moving. The striped animal was standing directly in front of him, its head turned away as it pointed its nose to the breeze. Its tail draped down behind it, and he could see the weight of it bending the tops of the grass. The markings on its flanks stood out clearly against the buff color of its coat. It seemed, this close, slightly smaller than he remembered it, thinner and sleeker and, from the way it stood, more furtive, more evidently a hunter. He could see how it was made for running, its legs thick and strong and sprung on wedged shoulders and a muscular rump. Alive, it looked much more capable of staying so.

It lowered its muzzle near the earth and released something it was carrying, some leftover of a meal that flopped into the leaf litter and stayed where it was laid. The animal yawned then, and its jaws opened and opened impossibly far, so its chin might have touched its chest. They snapped shut again with a neat click of teeth. Its ears were pricked but did not shift to register the sounds the animal heard. It slung its neck low and sniffed at the thing it had dropped to the earth: then it jerked its head up and, to Satchel's surprise, gave several quick, guttural barks. The sound was taken in by the scrub and became that of branches cracking, of trees creaking, of rocks rolling, of tough, wind-slashed leaves.

Then it swung its head and looked over its shoulder at him.

It reacted with spectacular speed, leaping in an electrified bound some distance away. There, it spun to face him and he saw it front-on for the first time, the two large slanting ebony eyes centered above a jet, angular nose, the head smoothly flattened on top and rounded at the jaw. It had a ridge of darker hair running past its ears and down its muzzle, and there was a smattering of lighter fur smeared across its chest. It stared at him without blinking and he stared back at it incredulously. *Tiger*, he thought stupidly. *You, Thylacine.*

The grass shivered, and both Satchel and the animal dipped their glance to the noise. A small creature was pawing at the dust, and even in the shroud of the evening, the stripes along its spine were clear, and Satchel caught his breath. When he looked away from the pup, its mother's eyes were watching him. He could pick it up, he knew, and she seemed to know it too. He was the nearer, and she was afraid. He rose cautiously on an elbow and the tiger shifted uneasily, but she would not leave until she saw what happened to her infant, and he did not know immediately what to do.

It was a healthy, stocky young animal: she had been able to feed it well and it was too big for any pouch her slim body might conceal. Like all baby animals it was chubby in places that would eventually be sharpened: its muzzle and cheekbones, its legs and its paws. Its coat was downy and looked soft to the touch. It was gazing bewildered all around itself, wobbling to its feet in search of its mother, and when it turned its head toward him, he saw its straight, pointy whiskers. He could lean across and touch it, if he wanted: he could slide a palm under its belly and lift it with one hand. He could take it home and change his world once again.

He pushed himself slowly upward until he was

crouched on his knees, and as he moved, he watched the tiger, who stayed perfectly still. He wondered if she was thinking or if she was simply observing what would happen, passively accepting her fate. He suddenly decided against that, for the thylacine was a creature who defied destiny. Against terrible odds it had saved itself: it had sidestepped extinction. It had found a trap-door.

And now the beast was looking at him, and one lay vulnerable within the reach of his hand.

If he found a thylacine, his life would never be the same. He remembered what Chelsea had talked about, the money and the glory. But his life wasn't going to be the same anyway, because things were already changed. If he found a thylacine, people could forgive themselves for some of the things they'd done. They would look at a caged creature and see in it redemption for themselves. He remembered the photographs he had seen of the last captive tiger imprisoned in the barren cell of a zoo. It had stayed close to the wire and it had died there alone. That was not the way for a survivor to live.

He had no right to take its gift for survival and use it for himself. In the end, the only thing that would help him would be something he already owned.

"Thylacine," he whispered, and the striped animal raised her head slightly, listening to him. But he found he had nothing else to say to it; he couldn't think of any words. He didn't actually think it proper, for something like him to speak to something like it. He unfolded his legs carefully, finding his feet without haste. The thylacine tensed but did not hedge farther away. He looked down at the little tiger. He longed to touch it, to ruffle the fluffy hair of its throat and run his hand over the sickle-shaped marks on its spine. But he did nothing, worried that if he touched it, its mother would not want it back.

He stepped away, one step after another, until he was as far from the pup as was the thylacine herself. "There," he said, "he's yours. I won't take him from you."

But she didn't twitch: she watched him, and every few seconds her deep eyes returned to the creature in the grass. So he moved away farther, and in moments the pup was lost from his sight. By the time the thylacine trod hesitantly through the clearing, he could scarcely see her either, but he saw her bow her head and collect the precious burden she had left in the dirt and he saw her flit away lightly, gone before he realized.

He stood still for ages, not knowing what to do. He was standing, he realized, in utter darkness, and he could only see at all because the pitch had snuck in unnoticed around him. He felt dazed by what had happened, and beneath that he felt a tremendous, soaring joy. His mind had ceased its awful whirling, and he felt alive and unafraid. He discovered he was smiling, that he was churned with exultation and he wanted to laugh and yell. He would describe the feeling to William and tell his father that he was not wrong: sometimes, something godlike did provide. He would go to the ocean and throw his fate into the sea.

It was dark now, and a good time to go home. He walked along the track and, impatient, he began to run, never stumbling in the blackness because, like an animal, he could see.